True Life Nude

by Suki

Naked Eye Publishing

First published online at truelifenude.co.uk 2015
Naked Eye edition published 2019

Book design and typesetting by Naked Eye
Cover illustration by Phil Moody/Sue Vickerman

ISBN-13: 9781910981092

www.nakedeyepublishing.co.uk

How has Suki ended up in Berlin, and why isn't it working out? After last year's stillbirth and the damp squib of her first novel's publication, leaving England was meant to be a fresh start, both for her writing and her love-life; an attempt to pick up the threads with her ex, Ilka.

Just like it was back home, life-modelling to earn her crust has become her mainstay here in Berlin. Thus, far from being a change, it's proved to be same old, same old. Berlin is depressing. Ilka is depressing. Suki's current manuscript lies untouched - and she's feeling fat.

But suddenly, out of the blue, ex-fling Tamara back home has fixed Suki up with some exotic photographic modelling… Furthermore, a surprise text from enigmatic acquaintance Bel is offering an adventure in Shanghai! New worlds beckon. The choice to move on is the easy part. *Running away again*, says Ilka…

Is Suki incapable of love – or are people around her just difficult? Can she survive the bleak isolation of her new situation? Will Suki and her latest fellow-traveller manage to move on to a happier place – together? The final phase in Suki's journey is to prove by far her greatest challenge.

Suki's creator Sue Vickerman has received three Arts Council (UK) awards for her poetry, novels and short stories. An international readership has followed Suki's serialised trilogy which may be read at sukithelifemodel.co.uk. Part I, A Small Life, is additionally available in print (Cinnamon Press) as is part II (Naked Eye Publishing). Part III, True Life Nude, concludes the trilogy.

Also by Sue Vickerman

Poetry

Shag
Arrowhead Press, England, 2003
Naked Eye, England, 2015

The social decline of the oystercatcher
Biscuit Publishing, England, 2005

Kunst by 'Suki'
Indigo Dreams Publishing, England, 2012

Thin bones like wishbones by 'Suki' and Sue Vickerman
Indigo Dreams Publishing, England, 2013

Adventus
Naked Eye, England, 2018

Fiction

Special needs, Cinnamon Press, Wales, 2011

A small life, Cinnamon Press, Wales, 2012

Two Small Lives, Naked Eye Publishing, England, 2015

Online fiction

asmalllife.co.uk

twosmalllives.co.uk

truelifenude.co.uk

Blog

sukithelifemodel.co.uk

Acknowledgements

I am grateful to the following photographers for permitting me to use their work in this story. The photographer-characters in the story are entirely fictitious, bearing no resemblance in any respect to the providers of these photographs, with two exceptions: the photograph taken by UK artist Tom Wood, and two photographs by Colombian artist David Rodriguez.

Mike Kilyon provided images for the characters of: Bel, Mike Little, Hong Kong Ron.
mikekilyon.co.uk

Lloyd Spencer provided images for the character of Aussie Cyril.
flickr.com/people/lloydspencer
theheartofleeds.com

Phil Moody provided images for the character of Fei Mo Di.
philmoody.com

Douglas Black provided images for the character of Greg-I'm-a-Kiwi.
dougalterego.blogspot.co.uk
facebook.com/junglemunkey

Tom Wood - see the photo used for 3rd April.
tomwoodartist.com

Lois Brothwell provided images for the character of Loiza.
loizart.co.uk

David Rodriguez - see the photos used for 26th March and 31st March.
art-davidrodriguez.com

Rod Jackson provided images for the character of Jacques-from-Brussels.

True Life Nude is a work of fiction in which no character represents any living person.

Contents

PART I

A new beginning

11th September
Friday morning, lying in bed

Last night's epiphany is making me face facts.

Trying to patch things up with Ilka has been desolate. The truth is, three months in, my Berlin adventure has gone pear-shaped.

So has my body.

That's why I can't write - even with *Über*agent Victoria Herz of Brown and Herz Literary Agency champing at the bit for my second novel. Just thinking about my unfinished manuscript makes me shrivel up and open another bloody bottle of champagne.

And Acquiescent Ilka lets me.

As for the life-modelling that earns my crust, I've had it up to here. Berlin's artists are as up themselves as British ones.

Why do people want to draw me - a fellow creature - naked, subdued, uncomfortable in an arduously lengthy pose? Is it after all, as the Po-faced Feminists would have it, exploitation? Abuse? The problem isn't the nakedness. I'm talking about the lack of heed for the model's wellbeing.

Whereas last night's session was something else. A different kind of artist; a different kind of art. A careful, controlled way of relating. Yes – *care*-ful. Full of care.

Though the Po-faced Fs would have kittens.

At six pm I got an international call from my ex-flingette in Leeds, Tamara: 'Get yourself to Szredski Strasse asap, Cafe Dezember. Go straight down to the basement. I've booked you a session with a Shibari bondage master.'

You have to submit to Tamara. Everyone does.

Turns out Tamara was paying Ron the photographer (a pal from her Hong Kong days) to send her the resulting pictures.

Thank god Ilka is in Leipzig with her work. She gets back tonight. Bondage would appal her. Because Ilka's a hard-liner: men subdue women. The patriarchy spoils her day. Her position has remained immutable these thirty years. She's stuck in the 'eighties Women's Movement past. Whereas I've gradually become became male-curious. They are interesting. For instance, the most common cause of death for men under fifty is suicide. We women think we've got problems? Men have certainly got problems.

Already so many impossible things before breakfast.

Ping! A text.

Hey - wow - from Enigmatic Bel! How long has it been?

And what a proposal!

Photographer: **Hong Kong Ron**

Shibari is a Japanese artistic form of rope bondage originating in an ancient martial art for the restraint of captives. The master who tied me up in this and other poses last night - hired by Just-Do-As-I-Say Tamara - was brilliant. A real expert.

An epiphanic night, and now this! Are the gods intervening, on this September morning in Ilka's sparse, frugal apartment off Prenzlauer Allee?

11th September
Still Friday, a bit later

> *Come on a 3-month tourist visa in first instance, stay in this flat w/ me (uni campus) & write. I cn get you plenty cash-in-hand wrk as Art Nude photographic model, eg Shanghai Art Nude Grp. No more 2-hr poses in freezing Berlin cellars! Bel*

I'm at the breakfast table, still in shock, re-reading Bel's text. Shanghai!!! God, it would be amazing. And her promise of photographic work is uncanny, because what I learned in last night's session is that contemporary Art Nude photography is not necessarily blokes photographing gorgeous birds naked. Was it ever?

But… Bel. This weird photographer woman. She's really nice but she barely speaks. We got friendly due to her project making fly-on-the-wall docu-movies of artists at work in life-rooms where I had bookings. But not *that* friendly… What do I know about her? Her website says she used to be a photo-journalist in places like Afghanistan, but that career seems to have abruptly ended. A bad experience? A nervous breakdown? I think she's got Post Traumatic Stress Disorder or something. I once spotted her leaving my psychotherapist's office as I was on my way in.

And how old is she - fifty? Older? Early-retired? Her photography blog divulges nothing about family, hometown, partners, early life…

Why invite me? Does she consider us close?

Hey - an email from Hong Kong Ron! *You can view the photos from last night via Dropbox.*

Dozens of images…

I prop my iPad on the table for a good browse, shifting aside Ilka's current reading-matter - an article by Susan Sontag (late partner of fantastic New York photographer Annie Leibowicz) in which Ilka has underlined some words in red pen:

At my afternoon session in Prenzlauerberg, an obese artist paints me huge-bellied. Bastard - leaning over his grotesque gut to reach his canvas. But the artist beside him is worse, copying the drawing method of tediously mechanical Euan Uglow, who in turn honed his technique, according to a thing by Adrian Searle in The Guardian[2], under the tutelage of equally anal William Coldstream. These guys compute the information the eye receives then reproduce the human form with the technical precision of a surveyor's plotlines.
   Passionless.

'To photograph something is to appropriate it.'
Yawn. Feminist analysis is *so* single-track. I mean, Hong Kong Ron's images are sensual, sexy, but that doesn't mean he has 'claimed ownership' of me. They portray submission, trust, intimacy, ecstasy, pain, beauty. There is texture, geometry, intricacy. They are Art.

Why did Tamara set this up? She must still want me! I was the one who, in running off to Berlin, ended our brief flingette: a hedonistic riot of sex - her dominating, me submitting (amid our screeches of laughter) - conducted in the windows her crazy schedule allowed. Tumultuous fun and pleasure. Which is impossible, of course, to sustain in a long-term relationship.
Or not?

Afternoon. My weekly session at the *Volkshochschule*. I get into pose, and into my head. My first musing: why do am I submitting to being mapped; turned into an architect's plan? Whereas last night's submission - both to the rigger and the photographer - was by contrast *so-o* sympathetic. The Master and Hong Kong Ron were humane towards me – to my body – in a way that too many artists are not.

But on to the newly urgent issue. I must look at my three options:
1) stay in Berlin with Ilka. Get fatter. Get more depressed. Never have a laugh. Never write again.
2) Shanghai! Amazing… But I think Bel's got issues, and I'm rubbish at dealing with mental health (scares me).
3) Return to UK. Write books living with Tamara. Let her dominate me, tell me what to do (I need that); make me shut up and listen (no mean feat), kneel at her feet, obey her… I love all that. Maybe "fun" really can be permanent!

Back in the flat, Ilka is home and making hummus. We watch a documentary about German reunification issues. We don't talk.

12th September
Saturday night with Bader Meinhof

Ping - a text comes through in my break. Tamara! Her first communiqué in the 48 hours since that bondage session she so masterfully set up.

Pics show u likd it. My man Ron & rigger more attentive to yr wellbeing than fcking artists yes? Overt & honest D/s. Fab.

D/s? I'll google that later. I shoot off my answer.

Yes, very *fab. Plannin return to UK. Yu still require live-in maid?*

But by the end of the session I've received the following response:

Bugger. Soz, Suki. Jus movd in wid sick father, ex astronaut, 86, Guernsey. Cancer, prognos 6 mths, cd b 2 yrs, he fights! I love my dad. Precious time. My needs 2nd place.

Bugger bugger bugger bugger bugger bugger.

Gloomy homeward tram-ride through Prenzlauerberg's autumnal September night. My booking has been in an old-established *Wohngemeinschaft* – a commune of anarchist artists with a fabled historical link to Bader-Meinhof - in a squatted former bread factory near Hackescher Markt. Their "studio" is the cellar – unheated, damp, gothic, mausoleum-esque - whose white-tiled vaulted caverns stretch labyrinthine under the railway...

I turned blue with cold, but that lot were too up themselves to notice. I hate my life.

Aldi Supermarkt on the ground floor of Ilka's building offers a procrastinatory distraction. I pick up the cheap *Sonderangebot* champagne – the cause of my belly's repulsive bulge. Mentally I'm revisiting the Cafe Dezember's specially-equipped basement. Suspended on a handmade rope from the 19th century ceiling I slowly spin. Helpless. Ecstatic.

But it's getting late. I must drag myself up the stairs to Ilka's apartment. To Ilka.

'*Shanghai*?' Ilka, just in from Lesbian Bicycle Maintenance, slaps her cycle helmet down on the kitchen table.

'I'm sorry I ever came to Berlin,' I continue.

'You'd stay with that weird photographer woman?...'

'Be honest, Ilka: it hasn't worked out. This second attempt. Anyway how was your workshop?

'...the one who barely speaks!'

'I'm not managing to write here, Ilka.'

'You don't know anything about her...'

'Bel and I get on very well. We made all those film shorts together.'

'You think she's got undiagnosed Post-Traumatic Stress Disorder.'

'We've all got our issues. Look - I'm not doing anything here.'

'You are! You've been modelling!'

'I'm *not writing*.'

'But you've only been here three months.' Ilka pulls off her jacket and beanie, slumps onto a stool. 'You'd be running away again.'

'I'm losing sight of my *raison d'etre*. It's making me scared. And I'm getting fat.'

Silence.

'So anyway... I'll be sleeping on the sofa tonight.' I hate myself for upsetting her. 'Want some champagne? There's an opened one in the fridge.'

And so at last, after a roller-coaster day and a half, I text Bel my response to yesterday's momentous offer.

SHANGHAI HERE I COME more details pls!

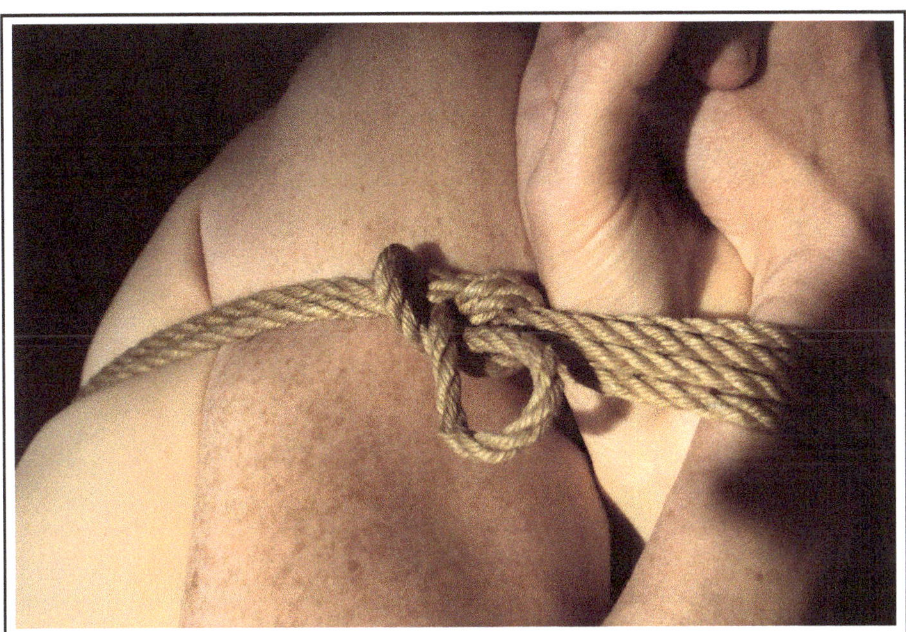

Photographer: **Hong Kong Ron**[3]

Another photo from my amazing Shibari bondage session here in Berlin. The whole new world of Art Nude photography beckons…

13ᵗʰ September
The early hours of Sunday

1.15 a.m. sees me in my sleeping bag on Ilka's sofa, face pushed up against her book-case, sleepless. Betty Friedan, Germaine Greer, Anais Nin, Laura Mulvey, Simone de Beauvoir's *Das Andere Geschlecht*, Sexism and God-talk, *Was Wollen die Frauen?* by Susie Orbach and Luise Eichenbaum, Fear of Flying. I pick out one by Karen Kleinfelder because it was published in 1993, two decades on from some of those old-hat feminists.

It turns out to be a criticism of Picasso's sexual way of relating to the model. It is poppycock: a total throw-back to the 1960s 'male gaze' debate initiated by feminist academic Laura Mulvey, a thing Bel educated me about soon after we met (was that four years ago already?).

Tamara says the 'male gaze' theory is dead. If models suffer *vis-a-vis* their artist employers, the gender relationship isn't the crux of the problem. Inter-personal relationships are absolutely - says Tamara - about power, but nowadays, let's be honest, we are likely to have chosen our roles. Dominant. Submissive.

Ping!

I was almost asleep. It's Bel, answering my hyper-enthusiastic *Shanghai here I come!*

Great! Want 2 photograph u, explore some ideas. Been thinkin of dis 4 ages, I did Art Nude photog at Slade tho ended up photo-journalist (hence teachin photog/media here). Big Lee Miller fan - final-yr thesis ws abt her – she gets lost in Man Ray's shadow

So Bel's invite is because she wants to photograph me! Why not a lovely Chinese girl? She must have some gorgeous students?

And who is Lee Miller? I remember vaguely, one time when Bel and I were both on trips to London, she texted me suggesting we go to a Lee Miller exhibition somewhere. But I was busy.

I search on my i-Pad. *One of the most stunningly beautiful, liberated women of the 20th century.* Fashion model. Art Nude model. Genius. Alcoholic. Depressive. Free-thinker. Liberated. *Too* liberated: she posed for an advert for sanitary towels in 1929 that ruined her fashion-modelling career. Also fashion photographer, and - aha! - war photographer.

Was it Lee Miller who inspired Bel to go as a photo-journalist to Afghanistan?

This finely-detailed original mono-print shows artist and model – Janey and me – juxtaposed in a similar position to the artist and model figures appearing in Picasso's famed late series (produced from the 1950s till his death) which show a female (usually) model juxtaposed with an increasingly decrepit and grotesque artist. This series is the subject of an epic thesis by feminist academic Karen Kleinfelder who says these images make us *'voyeurs of voyeurism':* we witness (in observing the artist at work) the desire to possess; thus we ourselves enjoy the fantasy of possession of the object – which is, of course, the woman.

Doh.

Furthermore (declares Ms K), *'the overwhelming carnality or physicality about his late paintings* [prove that the model] *remains from start to finish the object of the* [...] *male gaze* [...] *motivated by his "macho" need to affirm the power of his own penetrating gaze over the female figure,* [his gaze thus taking on] *an explicitly phallic connotation'.'*

Look, Karen. What exactly is supposed to be wrong about Picasso, or any of us, representing our sexuality through art-making? You yourself perceive in his work sexual aggression towards the model, but others don't. You say the artists he depicts hold their palettes and brushes near their groins – *'a substitute for an erection'*; the paintbrush always poised over the model's genitals *'implying penetration'*. If so, so what?

And what about when the artist-*voyeur* of the female model is also female? Is that still problematic? Would you, Ms K, define my relationship with Janey as one of sexual domination and submission (or, as Tamara has taught me, 'D/s')?

I can't be bothered with this nonsense.

Artist **Janey Walklin**

28th September
Monday - the day before my flight!

'She fancies you, right?'

I am ramming underwear into my suitcase's remaining nooks and crannies.

'Ha ha. Dunno if she's even a dyke.'

'She wouldn't have invited you otherwise.'

'She wants me for an Art Nude photographic project.'

'Photography isn't Art.'

'I can't believe you said that! The "photography isn't Art" debate is anachronistic, tired and anyway stupid.' (Pause) 'Okay I read that.[5] But it's what I think.'

Things have deteriorated between us. A fortnight of increasing bickering. Not my fault. Ilka has totally gone into hard-line mode, these days.

She retorts obstinately - 'As Susan Sontag said, paintings and drawings of an image are considered to be interpretations whereas photographed images are viewed as miniatures of reality. i.e. documentary, not Art.'

'I read that article! I think you'll find she goes on to say that photos are still interpretations.' I will win this argument. I fetch the book from the top of the fridge where it got tidied to, turn to the article[6] and start (loudly) reading out bits. 'See: *interpretations… shaped and formulated by tacit imperatives of taste and conscience…*'

Ilka of course turns away. 'Whatever, Suki. As far as I'm concerned, photography is just another imposition of male supremacy and control.'

'That comment is straight from the joyless, outdated feminism of your bookcase. Look at Lee Miller – she was *totally liberated* as a model! Right back in, like, 1920! Like, totally free in her sexual behaviour and attitudes. Multiple lovers and stuff. Polyamorous. I mean, even nowadays most people are possessively monogamous, but she wasn't. Polyamory is still even today associated with kink rather than being what the mainstream wants.'

Stony silence from Ilka.

I persist in having the final word. Even though it's stupid. 'That 'male gaze' theory, the one that says all the looking in the world is from men's viewpoint and for their exclusive pleasure - it's so 1970s. It's so *over*.'

Ilka is now by the door. 'Suki, I've got an overnight in Leipzig again. A work thing. So I won't be here tomorrow when…'

'Good. Coz we hate goodbyes, don't we.'

The door closes behind her.

Tsk. She has never once stood up to me.

…Does Bel fancy me?

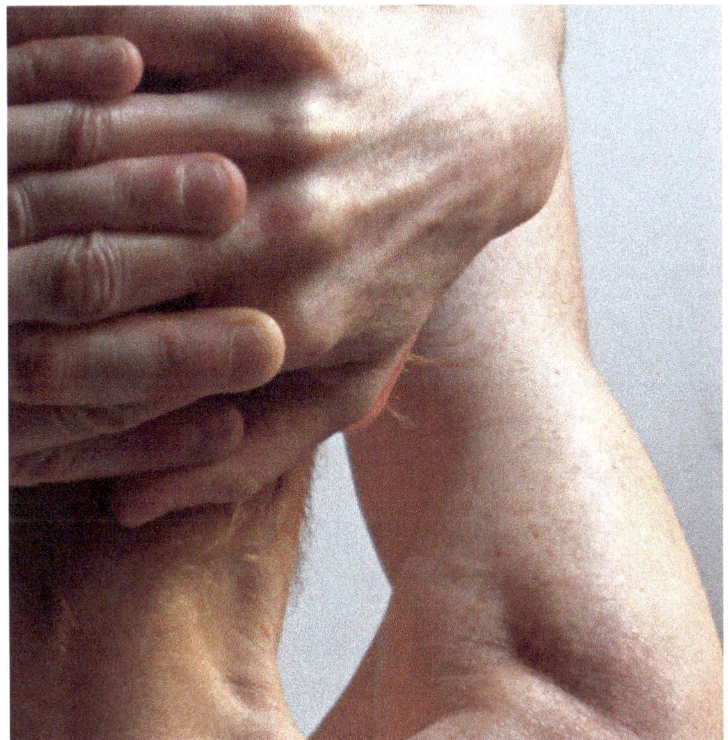

Photographer: **Bel**

Bel took this pic in my old flat while we were making a movie she called 'Suki's Life Room'.

Here's the Susan Sontag quote I battered Ilka with:
  'In deciding how a picture should look; in preferring one exposure to another, photographers are always imposing standards on their subjects. The 1930s photographers of the 'Farm Security Administration' [blah blah blah] …took dozens of pictures of their sharecropper subjects until satisfied with the precise facial expression that supported their own notions about poverty, light, dignity, texture, exploitation, and geometry…'

29th September
Tuesday - the early hours

Berlin to Shanghai - out of the frying pan into the fire?

I am in my sleeping bag, nose-to-nose one last time with Ilka's bookcase.

I haven't been able to sleep.

I scan her books for something - anything - post-feminist; none of this po-faced anti-sex nonsense. Karen Kleinfelder's tome has been replaced in its alphabetically rightful slot. I leaf through it again: maybe her erudition will helpfully put me to sleep.

> *'…any representation that explicitly thematizes the act of representation is self-referential twice over, the act of representation playing a dual role as both signified and signifier…'*

I used to have patience with this type of deep analysis, but isn't it premised in a kind of optimistic belief in our layers and layers of sophistication as humans? Doesn't age and maturity bring the realisation we're simply animals?

Or am I just getting lazy in my old age?

Whatever. I use a pen lying on the bookshelf to mark the text so that Ilka might one day be entertained by it.

'Are you defacing my book?'

'Ilka! God – you made me jump! No, not defacing. Just asterisking some bollocks.'

Ilka grins - 'Still wanting to educate me' - yet looks deeply sad. She flops onto my sleeping-bagged feet. Her raincoat is wet. Her hand lands on the hump of my knee.

'Thought you were staying over in Leipzig! Why have you come home?'

'Because it's the end of our story. Because we have to say goodbye. Because I'm worried about you. Because we're both going to be lonely again.'

(Lonely? *Lonely?* I've been so lonely living with you, Ilka). I point at the page I'm on. 'This woman's entire thesis is based on her perception of

Picasso's creativity as being *exploitative* sexual activity. Da da da... here: the *'familiar theme of art-as-creative-rape-of-the-model'...'*

Ilka takes me by the shoulders. 'You're such a crap listener.'

Will she - for once - give me a good shaking? Lay down the law? Isn't that what I need?

But then she lets go again. Looks at her hands. 'Are you going to have one of your so-called "fling-ettes" with Bel?'

'Tsk! God's sake, Ilka. I'm going to Shanghai to *write my novel.*'

'Why can't you just stay still and love somebody? Relationships are hard work. You have to stick at them. Please, Suki. Change your mind. Please.'

Photographer: **Bel**

Bel took this photo for the cover of my poetry collection 'Thin Bones Like Wish-bones'. When I think about it, we've done a lot together. Maybe we *are* pretty good friends.

In the footnote I asterisked to show Friederike what rubbish Kleinfelder's book is, Ms K rejects curator Lise Vogel's benign suggestion that Picasso 'has a certain sensitivity to the nature of contemporary social and sexual relations'.[7]

'*Traitor!*' yells Ms K (okay, my *précis*). And she is even more offended by Vogel's implied criticism of the pervasive feminist view that all creative work *'is essentially equivalent to sex from the standpoint of a man, with the ever-present implication that such endeavours are perhaps not quite so valuable, so virile, as a good fuck.'*

Kleinfelder: *'How* dare *you let Picasso and all these other bastards off the hook!'* (My paraphrase again).

So what if Picasso's *oeuvre* demonstrates - from his male standpoint - that sex is a motivator of creativity? Why is that actually a problem? Let men be men, Karen.

Have I become an anti-feminist?

Berlin Schönefeld Airport. Grey rain, autumnal chill.

'Welcome on board.' The air hostess smiles, looking at me curiously. My eyes are still swollen from crying.

My flight is with Aeroflot. Cheap. Over-long. Thirteen hours hours to contemplate my fate.

On my lap is my half-read biography by Caroline Burke of Lee Miller, Man Ray's so-called "muse" in the nineteen-thirties. In the month since my epiphanic Shibari session, and in view of the project Bel wants to carry out, I've been googling Art Nude photography, and have thus collected interesting reading-matter and online documentaries for my new adventure.

We taxi down the runway.

First I will prime myself by watching *Ways of Seeing*. I have uploaded onto my newly-bought i-Pad all four episodes of this 1972 TV series by Mr. Right-On New Man John Berger. The Youtube review says it *'challenged and changed a whole nation'*. Apparently Berger has become famous for saying, *'Women watch themselves being looked at'*; as in, women are taught to think of themselves as always on view. But this is the twenty-first century. Men, too, are on view now – aren't they?

I put in my earphones...

Moscow airport. Awaiting my connection I check emails. One from Ilka already! My eyes well up again, but it turns out to be annoying.

> *Just visited Bel's website. She got fixation on yu, see pics on homepage. Be worried.*

> *Dear Ilka, Yes, tankyu 4 askin, journey going fine. Re Bel's pics of me – they from when she made those film shorts, just by-products. Hav nice day.*

I'm being made to defend Bel.

Is Ilka jealous?

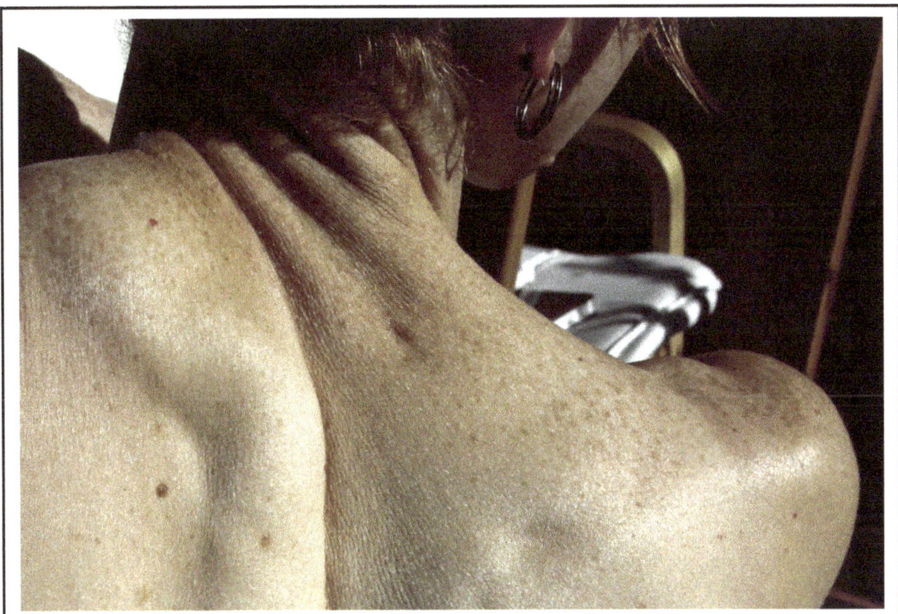

This pic appears on Bel's website *bel-photography.co.uk*. I don't believe that it is evidence (as Ilka would have it) of Bel "having a fixation" on me.

Last leg. Moscow to Shanghai. The plane is taxi-ing.

Clunk. Seatbelt on. My nose back in that biography. Lee Miller was only Man Ray's lover/"muse" for three years – so why is it made out to be her main claim to fame? Frivolous model, or professional photographer? Despite her son's posthumous promotion of her photographic and journalistic achievements, it seems images *of* her are more known than images *by* her.

Zzz… zzz…

Shanghai Pudong Airport. A day ahead: Wednesday already!

Sudden overwhelming humid heat. China. Fuck. *Fuck.*

Long sleek black hair… Short skirts… Smooth skinny legs… Who would ever give a man a second look? Bel could surely get some gorgeous Chinese girl for this project. Why does she want me?

Eventually, at the other side of a striped barrier, I see her. Creased linen shirt and slacks. Looks hot and sticky. Every bit the pasty British expat teacher.

I don't feel attracted to her. I just don't. Ought I to?

The awkwardness of having to work out how to greet each other is avoided - thank god - by the gushing of a pretty, beaming young girl:

'Welcome you! My name is Miss Lily Hong' – she holds out her name-card to me with both hands. Assistant vice-manager Foreign Affairs Department.'

'Hello – "Lily Hong", was that? *Ni hao!*'

1st October
Thursday – first morning in China!

'Good morning.' Gravely Bel hands me a cup of green tea in bed.

'Bloody hell I'm in Shanghai!' I pinch my own arm, laugh, a bit over-hearty; watch this strangely colourless, solemn woman, quite tall, average build, shoulder-length unstyled grey-flecked hair…

Aren't the best photographers this nondescript kind, the type of personality who manages to be fly-on-the-wall, invisible?

Bel is shoving apart the rickety sliding screens to the balcony.

'Are they supposed to prevent mosquitos getting in?' I show my blotchy arms. Alongside our beds – two singles jammed side by side in this teeny room – is an untidy stack of books. 'Hey, wow, these are all on Lee Miller – I've just read her biography!'

Bel, texting on the balcony, only nods – wordless, grey; the world beyond her also grey: scaffolded half-built tower blocks, pylons, more tower blocks, then the exotic silhouettes in the hazy distance of some of the world's most awesome skyscrapers. Is Bel secretly texting a friend – *Jeezus, why did I invite Suki here?*

Is there a sun, somewhere up above?

What the hell am I doing here?

Don't panic. I grab and flick through the first book off the pile.

When Bel comes back in I do a big beam. She brings her i-Pad over and props it up on my shrouded knees, and points at an on-screen graph. 'The government issues warnings when the Air Quality Index rating is over one hundred. Today looks like a good day; see - pollution report *"moderate"*. AQI only seventy-nine: *"Respiratory symptoms will only be experienced by people with unusual sensitivities"*.

'God!' My exclamation comes out with undue force. 'Everyone warned me about the pollution. Have you got "unusual sensitivities"?'

'Dunno really. I've been coughing a lot. It's worse in other places; they say breathing Beijing's air is the equivalent of smoking forty fags a day.[8] But it's bad here. Watch.'

She puts her palm down flat on the floor tiles, sweeps it sideways, shows me her upturned hand, the film of black smut. 'It's there every day, you can't keep on top of it.' She takes the book from me. 'This one's interesting because the writer talks about… let's see… the *'active-passive, male-female, photographer-model dichotomies that underlie most narratives of* [fashion] *photography…'*[9] which at first struck me as anachronistic – like, it no longer applies in the twenty-first century - but now I think maybe it *is* still true: this primitive Adam-and-Eve relationship does prevail – I mean, like, in fashion, in the photographer-model relationship, in lots of spheres. But the great thing is, Lee Miller subverted all of that – even back in the nineteen-twenties and 'thirties - by being both model and photographer, and by being so assertive and free…' Suddenly she stops, and for a single moment, her face shines. 'It's so great you're here!'

Hey - that must mean she's happy?!?

We set off to meet Lily Hong for breakfast in the staff canteen. I am led beneath the shade of ornamental trees across the grandiose, new-built faux-European college campus. Bel is in her default mode of solemnity again. 'The food in Shanghai is good. As long as you mentally blot out that food safety checks are corrupt, obviously. No point worrying about absolutely everything.'

Lily Hong is waiting like an excited puppy dog, a pink bow in her hair. 'Please take fried *jaozi.* Foreigners like very much.'

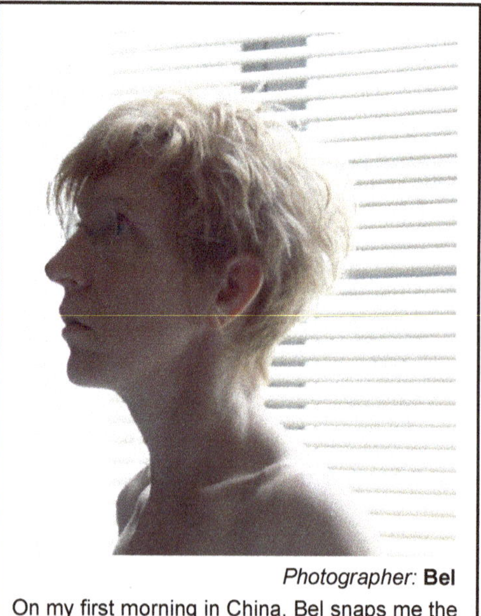

Photographer: **Bel**

On my first morning in China, Bel snaps me the moment I sit up in bed.

Beam. Squeeze of my arm. 'I like your hairs.' A pat on my head. She'll be licking my ankles next. Relief! Lily Hong definitely lightens the mood. Because being alone with Bel is no bundle of laughs.

I think of having a giggle and a drink with my upstairs neighbour Tiffany back home.

I don't know if I can hack this.

2nd October
Friday

It's stickily warm, despite being October.

'Wakey wakey! It's eleven thirty. I thought I'd better tell them you can do this afternoon's session because they only meet on the first Friday of the month.' Bel places a mug of green tea on the floor beside my bed.

'What? Who? What time? Yikes! Second full day in China and I'm already modelling!'

'It's Shanghai Art Nude Photographers' Group. You'll need that network to build up bookings. I'm sure you'll get some one-to-one sessions out of it.'

'God, I hope they don't mind these.' I hold out my blotched arms - the night's mosquito bites.

But Bel is focused on her iPad.

I scramble for the bathroom. 'So what will they want? I mean, how does it work? Should I take some ideas?'

Silence. I see she's engrossed in The Guardian newspaper online.

'Think I'll quickly print off some poses, see if they'd like me to copy them. Egon Schiele and Lucien Freud...' (no response from Bel) '...Could try some of those notorious Euan Uglow poses that hurt his models, coz that's the great thing about photographic modelling - you don't need to hold a pose for very long.'

A few minutes later Bel calls to me through the bathroom door. 'I'll help you set up a 'qq' email account before we go out so you can give out a contact address that works. Your gmail account won't work here. Google's blocked. Yahoo is sometimes blocked. They've started messing up Hotmail. All the non-Chinese servers get problems. It's easier to just give up and use the state-controlled one.'

Later, Bel leads me by the hand through the crowds. My second full-on blast of city life: from demolition site to half-built tower-block complex, lace-necked cranes rotating high above chaotic slums, to space-age subway, to old-world tree-shaded French Concession – and always, the seething masses of humanity that I can barely separate out into persons. Exhausting!

'...So I finish teaching at six – I'll see you in the flat. Cyril says he'll help you get a taxi. Show the driver this card. Hope it's good!' Bel leaves me with the men.

Yes - all men. Why am I not surprised? They are an exotic mix of races and accents aged from mid-twenties to retirement. The introductions are friendly: a rotund elderly Australian named Cyril, Jacques from Brussels, Fei Mo Di whose English accent is cut glass, several other orientals who may or may not be Chinese, a Kiwi, two north Americans - all successful enough to afford amazing photographic kit, and from a background that has enabled them to speak good English. Most are impossible to categorize anyone, with the exception of one familiar type who, before he jovially opens his mouth, has wife-kidsatuni-earlyretired-doing-abitof-consultancy written all over him.

'Mike Little from Swindon, for my sins! How d'you do.'

'I'm Suki. Hi.' I drop my rucksack and, to avoid some kind of big de-robing moment, instantly pull off my dress and wander about. Sweat beads on my ribby chest and runs down my inner thighs. I wipe off my face. The tissue turns grey: a fine paste made of humidity and pollution has coated my skin.

The photographers are already in a horseshoe, some with tripods, leaving a big open area in which I can work. The deal is, they'll each email me their best pics from the session.

Aussie Cyril, portly, avuncular, opens his arms as though preparing for a bear-hug. 'We've all agreed to let the new model take the lead.'

So I show them the Schiele, Freud and Uglow paintings I've printed off. There is courtesy, humour, and lots of movement – both on my part, and on the part of the enthusiastically snapping voyeurs. And certainly no pain.

Do I fancy any of them?

Do any of them fancy me?

Do they do shoots like this with male models?

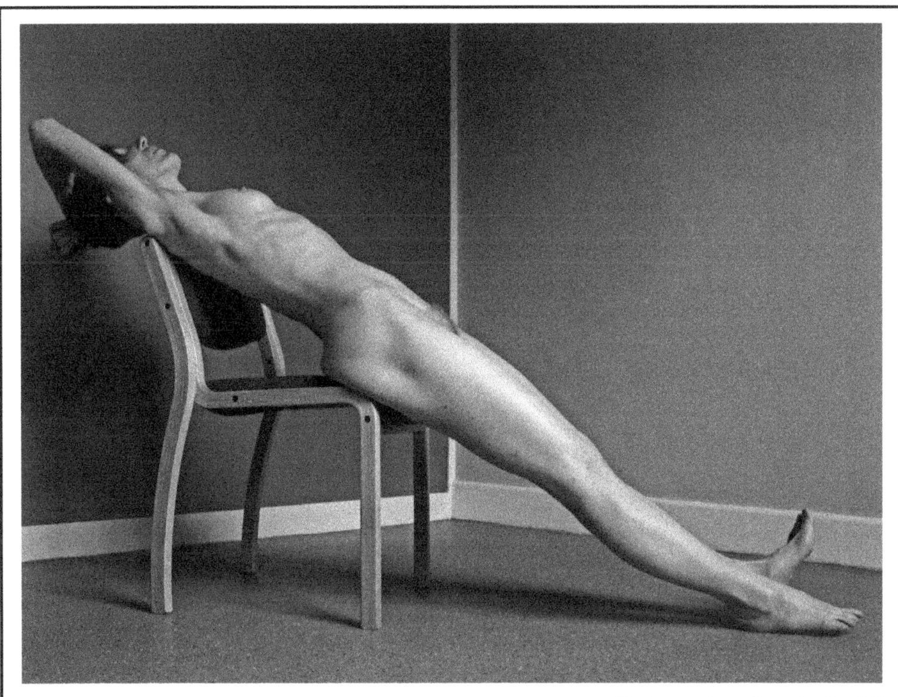

Aussie Cyril is the first photographer to email me a photo of this pose I did: a copy of one I call 'plank woman', famously painted by artist Euan Uglow.

16th October
Friday – two weeks in!

Mid-October and yet hot! (Well, at least by British standards).
   When will I finally start to write?
   Each day, while Bel goes teaching, I wander about - still "acclimatising". Staring. Being stared at. The street market was traumatic the first time I went alone. Now I stare through the cat-calls, grin back at the smiles. Great writing-fodder. It's just - all still too new.

Bel is as bad. When is she going to start this Art Nude project with me?
   Her morning coughing fits have become my alarm clock. Today the Air Quality Index reports only moderate pollution: *Unhealthy for people with special sensitivities. Asthmatics and the elderly may have difficulties.* But she coughs whatever the level, on her narrow bed next to mine, scowling at the news pages on her iPad.

Anyway. Got my first one-to-one booking for a photo-shoot! Fei Mo Di - he with the cut-glass English accent, crisply-ironed shirt and jeans.
   So here I am in his bright, white, twenty-fourth floor penthouse. The cityscape beyond the glass walls is a sci-fi movie-set. Vertiginous. Much of it in a state of semi-construction.
   He's only the second Shanghainese person I'm meeting really properly, after Bel's little assistant Lily Hong. But it turns out Fei Mo Di is not all that Chinese. He went to Eton, then the Central College of Fine Arts in Beijing, topped off with a Masters in New York. His mother is vice-chair of a metropolitan committee for culture or something, on the Communist Party's Consultative Council. She owns real estate in Kensington.
   I'm sipping from a tiny translucent cup. Just beyond the floor-to-ceiling window, the neck of a crane slowly approaches us. What if it doesn't stop? The elegant tea-set is on a huge perspex

desk beside an Apple computer. Fei Mo Di points at the monitor - his photos from the group session. 'I haven't sent you these yet. See - I was moving around you a lot, focusing in. So I want to do that again now. I'd like you quite simply, first of all, to stand absolutely still, statuesque.' He gets up, goes over to where lights are rigged up. 'Right here.'

I get into position. Silently he begins. What's the etiquette when one-to-one? Should I chat?

'Ahem. I'm really interested in whether art-photographers relate to their models differently from artists,' I begin.

No immediate reaction. Click, click.

'Like, whether there's a more natural, human relationship with a photographer? I mean, doesn't a photographer want somebody *alive*?'

Click. 'Yes.' Click. Click.

Was that curt? Should I say more? 'Whereas artists… I mean, Uglow, for example; he objectified his models to the extreme. He was so fanatical about the precise reproduction of what he was looking at that he'd actually measure out graph-lines on his studio wall and number them to mark *exactly* where the model was positioned. Flipping autistic!'

The tele-photo lens stares coldly. 'Autism has been known to equate with artistic genius.' The lens roams to my belly, comes in close to my left breast, shoulder…

'Well, but the crap way Uglow related to the model…'

Fei Mo Di cuts in. 'Are you familiar with the work of Chuck Close? He's an autistic man whose excruciatingly meticulous process creates astonishing paintings that happen to start from a photograph.'

'But if it's from a photograph it's not really Art' (okay, I argued the opposite point with Ilka, but this guy's Etonian accent is aggravating). I hammer on: 'A photo is conventionally believed to show "the real thing" whereas a painting holds greater interest and value because it's a unique and expressive interpretation through the artist's eye, because everyone knows

- and as Anaïs Nin said - "We do not see things as they are, we see things as *we* are".'

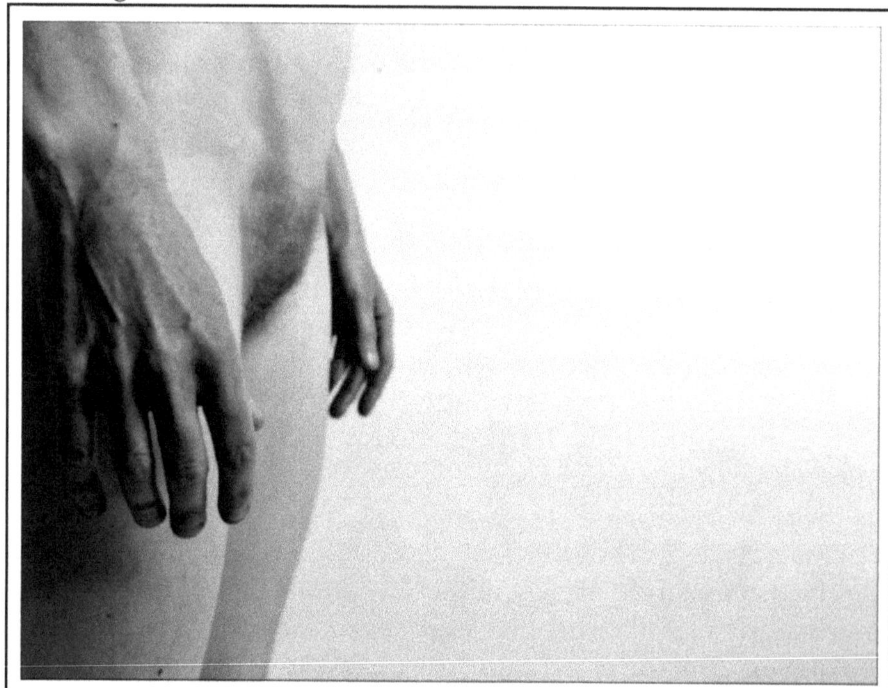

Photographer: Fei Mo Di[11]

At the Shanghai Art Nude Photographers group session, this guy Fei Mo Di spun off from the Uglow, Schiele and Freud poses I was doing, and did his own thing.

'Tuh. Glurge.' Snap, shift, snap.

'Pardon?'

'Your Anaïs Nin quote. Asinine.'

'That is *not fair*. People are always sticking the knife into Anaïs Nin. It's because she was a writer. Words on the page are explicit in a way that visual imagery isn't, so we're easier to criticize.'

Fei Mo Di looks round his camera at me, clearly annoyed.

'I'm a writer myself.' Standing there naked, I know I am ridiculous.

Late afternoon. The air downtown feels raspy on an in-breath. I flounce up to Bel who is waiting, as arranged, on the China Art Museum steps. 'Huh. Pompous git.'

'Fei Mo Di?' She puts out her cigarette; coughs. 'Your shoot didn't go too well, then?'

'He called Anaïs Nin a 'spoiled upper-crust adulteress'. Why does she get treated with such contempt? Lee Miller doesn't, even though her sexual conduct was just as liberated and controversial...' I follow Bel through the museum's entrance. 'It's because Anaïs Nin was a writer, that's why. Visual imagery is infinitely ambiguous - all about the viewer's perception – whereas the written word is a record of a thing perceived, and furthermore, is the writer's take on it – their analysis. So the writer's soul is laid bare. We're more vulnerable to deeply personal criticisms.'

Zero response from Bel. Which is usual. Does she think I talk rubbish? When a man ignores me I assume it's coz he's a sexist pig.

Do I talk rubbish?

The foyer is a huge modern space. A ruddy-faced immigrant from the countryside in cheap gaudy leggings is pointing out Bel and I to her toddler, as though we were cows in a field.

'Maybe I talked too much.'

Bel hands me an English-language leaflet about the current exhibition. 'Did you? That's interesting. When you model for artists you never utter a word.'

'But with a photographer there needs to be interaction, doesn't there? To find the poses.'

Checking the leaflet's map, Bel heads off. 'What did you think of his penthouse?'

I hurry after her. 'Oh my god. Space-age. Shiny high-tech everything. That whole district is so pristine, glittering, brand new. All those exclusive luxury tower blocks. Was there *ever* anything old there?'

'Shanghai isn't old. Pudong was all paddy fields twenty years ago. You should read JG Ballard. He spent his formative years in wartime Shanghai when it was pure anarchy, which is why everything he's ever written has an apocalyptic undercurrent. That's Shanghai. Those towers built for the elite remind me of his novel 'High Rise'. They spook me.'

Why does Bel only get animated about climate change, wars, and the end of the world? I don't like thinking about those things.

'Anyway' – I shift the subject back – 'I don't think he'll book me again. He definitely didn't fancy me, I know that much.'

'Fei Mo Di? Apart from being twenty years younger than you he's as gay as a French horn.'

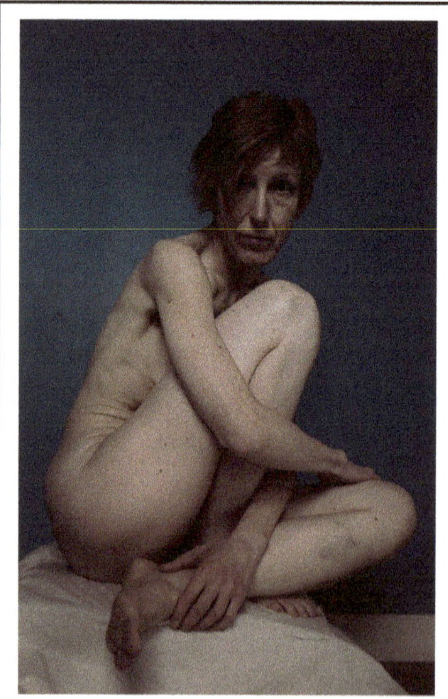

Photographer: **Aussie Cyril**

Another photo from the first Shanghai Art Nude Photographers group session. Aussie Cyril says it reminds him of the work of early photographer Ruth Bernhard. He has lectured in photography. He has a lot of knowledge.

We wander through the museum. Bel's and other visitors' pulled-off pollution-masks dangle against their chests, like surgeons taking coffee breaks.

I stop to field a Wechat message. 'Hey - another one-to-one booking! Next week. That elderly Aussie, Cyril.'

'Three times married.'

'God, Bel, your ex-pat world is incestuous.'

'He likes to submit to women. He's into kink.'

'How on earth do you…' -

- 'One of his exes told me. There's a lot of sex recreation in ex-pat Shanghai.' We have reached the central hall where the new exhibition is installed. Some are gigantic. 'Look! This is the fantastic stuff I wanted to show you. There's so much photography-based art here, of a kind you don't see in Europe.' Bel is animated again - this time about something positive, for once. Her sweeping arm takes in all the works: 'This isn't about photographs. Photographic techniques and media are merely tools in the creation of these works. This all goes way beyond the debate on whether a photograph can be considered art. I'm going to bring my students here.'

Enthusiasm! Wonderful. This is Bel's best moment since my arrival a fortnight ago. She's actually enjoying something.

I link my arm through hers. 'So. When are you going to start your Art Nude project with me?'

She immediately tightens a little. 'When are you going to get out your unfinished manuscript?'

12th November
Thursday

Week five of my Shanghai odyssey. A bright, warm afternoon.

Not long after leaving for the teaching block, Bel is back at the flat again.

'Thought you'd got photography undergrads this p.m.?'

She drops onto her bed. 'They've been sent out to sweep up the campus. Visit of dignitaries tomorrow.'

'God. So chaotic. The way things shift and change without notice.'

Bel already has her iPad in her hand.

'Well anyway, I'm sticking to my writing routine.' Pause. 'Do you want to come with?'

'It's alright. I'd like to just sit and catch up with BBC Online.'

'Right… I'll see you later.' She's obviously going to spend another afternoon being all depressively silent. I reach the door, look back from the threshold. 'You're addicted to those news sites,' I joke. 'All the world's bad news.'

I set out, like every afternoon, for the recently-opened Delightful Peony Coffee Home – the only cafe round here with a shop-sign and menu in English. The employees are migrants from the countryside with no English. The so-called lattes are made of condensed milk, served sweetened with syrup. Never mind. It's quicker and cheaper than trekking to a Starbucks in the city. And there is wifi.

I pick my way across the campus through gaggles of flirting students trailing the brooms with which they've been issued.

The gymnasium, not five years old, is already tatty, its pretend-redbrick tiles coming unglued from the exterior and dropping off in patches due to the damp creeping up its cement structure. Pudong's water table is barely subterranean. Dig six inches down and you're in a pool.

At the Delightful Peony I hook up to the WiFi. Damn. Today both the BBC and *The Guardian* newspaper are blocked. Techie Bel has yet to set me up with the illegal software everyone uses to get onto the web - a 'VPN'. But my Chinese 'qq' email account opens without a hitch. God – an answer from Aussie Cyril already. Is he pissed off? Pride made me want to show him my massively improved version of his photo – but not in person, in case of wrath.

Regarding the attached photo – I do not have a problem whatsoever with your changes, except that I am more than a little uncomfortable that the image now makes you look like the victim of the portrayer – a bit too 'apres Freud'! Discuss further tomorrow, still greatly looking forward. Very best wishes, Cyril Sent from my iPhone

When I get back to the flat Lily Hong is coincidentally, as on previous occasions, just leaving.

'This is always happening – it's uncanny!' I grin.

Bel calls out - 'English practice!' She comes over to the doorway. 'I've introduced Lily Hong to your autobiography on your website and we've been looking at your language notes for non-native-speakers.'

'I will read your stories Miss Suki – thank you!' Lily Hong flutters out, dimple-cheeked - 'Have a nice day! Don't worry be happy!'

I close the door behind her. 'Don't you find her a bit much? She's *so* frilly and effusive.'

'I'm grateful. She looks after me.'

Am I being criticised? 'Sorry – I'm crap at that. I'm deeply aware my only cooking contribution to this household is instant noodles. Bit of a liability, really. Bet you're sorry I came.'

'No! It's so great you're here,' she says, not looking at me. 'All those months when I was by myself… I was so lonely.' She takes my hand. Shock!

Is she being romantic? Oh my god; I don't… She's so…

'Uff.' I slip my hand from hers. 'Cuppa tea?'

Photographer: **Aussie Cyril**
My photoshopped version of one of Aussie Cyril's photos from the first group session (pose taken from a Lucien Freud painting). I rotated the image to make the curtain's edge a true vertical, removed the fabric's creases, cropped right to the edges of my body, and bleached out colour until I am sculpted marble - a bloodless creature into which *rigor mortis* has set. Good, or what?

13th November
The early hours of Friday

At one a.m. I am still at my makeshift desk (the chest of drawers in the bedroom). Behind me, Bel is on her bed asleep. I am delighted with my night's creativity. So what, if it's not writing creativity? This is *me* in these pictures: I claim the right to change my own look. I have my own ideas; I have the software to do it.

The only images I have not touched are the ones sent me by Fei Mo Di. His are perfect. Which seems amazing, considering we didn't like each other. Or maybe it's because of that? For him I am not a woman but a series of shapes, interestingly shaded. So what. He's just a French horn.

Am I disturbing Bel? She's not in deep sleep – I can tell from the breathing. Never mind – I'll quickly email my best result to Cyril. Maybe he's still up. Get his opinion.

Good evening Cyril –
First, re the crop I sent you of your 'apres Freud' pic - don't worry about me "looking like a victim". A victim of whom? I do this by choice. And just to let you know - you're not the only photographer whose work I am adulterating. I've been working on some of Jacques' photos. His shots of my Schiele poses were not at all Schiele-esque. Not edgy, not spiky, and (unlike some of yours) utterly unsexy. Attached is one of his I've drastically modified. Your thoughts?

Aussie Cyril must wear his cell-phone next to his heart. His response is almost instant.

Good evening to you, Suki! Your attached 'hand study' reminds me of some of Alfred Stieglitz's pictures of his model Georgia O'Keefe. I am looking forward to seeing more of your crops. Please tell me - which Art Nude photographers do you like? Yours, Cyril
sent from my iPhone

A sudden movement – Bel abruptly getting up. She sidles past to the toilet.

Is she pissed off? Have I kept her awake? I'll just shoot off a quick answer.

Don't really know any except Lee Miller, though she is more model and muse for Man Ray than photographer in her own right - yes? C u tomoz S

I turn off the lamp, go the bathroom after Bel has (wordlessly) returned, and clean my teeth. 'Ping!' - another email. Oh dear, I know she's annoyed but I just want to take a quick look. In the dark I creep back to the laptop.

My dear Suki, re Lee Miller, in my opinion she was a photo-journalist more than art photographer. If you will permit me, I would be delighted to regale you with some Art Nude history. I've got so many books I can lend you from my very extensive photographic library accumulated during many, many years of Media Studies lectureships, too many years, how can I be so old? (-: Luckily I have not yet begun the process of shipping them back to Australia. I think you'll find it interesting to look first at the Photo-Secessionist movement founded in 1902, led by Stieglitz. This is the movement that insisted on Art Nude photography becoming accepted as 'art'. I'll give you a book tomorrow. In fact it's already tomorrow, and time for a beauty to get her beauty-sleep, so I'll wish you goodnight! Sent from my iPhone

'That Cyril?'
I slide into my bed – 'yes.'
'Predatory.'

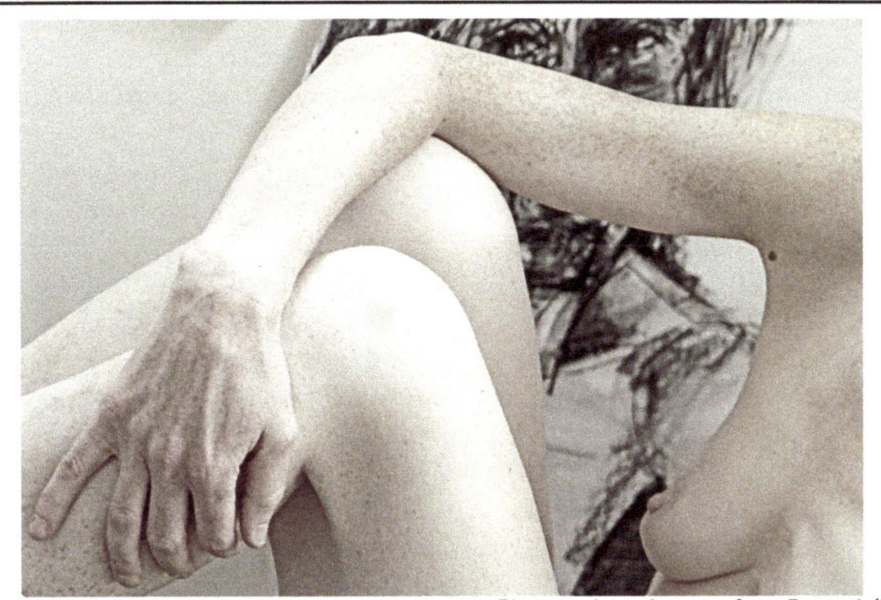

Aussie Cyril's permissiveness re: 'doctoring' his photographs has disinhibited me. I am re-visiting all the photos emailed to me by attendees of that first session with the Shanghai Art Nude Photography Group. I've cropped this pic by Jacques-from-Brussels to make it more of a hand study.

Friday *(continued)*

Yet another afternoon spent naked rather than novel-writing. Sigh. But it's money.

'I love women.' The eye of Cyril's small camera click-click-clicks, his plump lips smiling.

I adjust myself on Cyril's *chaise longue,* offering him a shoulder. 'Ah. No – I mean, my question was just in general terms. About how Art Nude photographers' ways of relating to their models have differed from the historical precedent of artists' relationships to their models.' I slither on the silk draperies, shift a cushion, stop again. 'I'm curious to find out if there's a difference.'

'Wait' - Cyril swaps the small camera for a chunky one with a vulgarly long lens, continues snapping: 'I don't think one can generalise. About either photographers or artists. Personally I photograph women because I love women. I would not want to photograph a male model. The very thought makes me shrink. Ooh, that's lovely. Absolutely lovely. More of that - yes - '

'That's so different from my experience of working with artists. We models are certainly not always loved. We're just a kind of tool. We just do as we're instructed.'

Cyril pauses at this, momentarily leaning on his oak panelling to look at me. 'Whereas I'll do anything you say.' Click, click, click.

'Erm … Is that - usual? The photographer led by the model?'

Click - 'that's terrific…' - click. 'My dear Suki, you'll find out that there have been very many Art Nude photographers and there's a great diversity of behaviours. But I reckon by and large the relationship to a model is an intimate and caring one.'

'Tuh. Whereas artists like Euan Uglow could work with a model for hours, days, months, years, and yet be absolutely disengaged from that human being. Like, one time a model died, so he just found another model with an identical physique and carried on with his painting! The model was a plank, not a personality. Why didn't he just bloody well take photographs, if he was that fanatical about precision recording? Or else why not just set up a technically challenging still-life? Why use a human?'

As Cyril drives me home his hand comes to rest too close to my thigh.

'Ahem' – I shift – 'I liked your use of drapes and sheets to get those varied backdrops. And your apartment's amazing.'

'I was very lucky to find that historic French Concession villa before real estate went through the roof.'

The fake grandeur of the new-built university campus looms ahead. 'Okay, this is my gate. Thanks, Cyril - it's been a really good session.'

He pulls in, and presses a thick wad of hundred yuan notes into my hand. 'Thank *you*, Suki, so very much' – he leans in, breathing heavily – 'I'd like to do many more shoots with you. Very very soon. *A bientot!*'

Before bedtime Cyril has already emailed today's pictures. I show Bel.

'He's out to make you pretty.' She walks off.

I agree. I don't like that either. But should I risk upsetting him by telling him? He pays so well.

*Tanx 4 these Cyril! My absolute fave of urs will always be de
Uglow plank-woman from de group session. Mus go bed now! S x
P.S. Btw tanx again 4 lending me books - have browsed Alfred
Stieglitz - some of his Georgia O'Keefe pics r like Bel's studies of
my hands n feet.*

I send Cyril this, then want to add a quick after-thought. I start another email.

*P.S. May I bring more Egon Schiele and Lucien Freud poses to our
next meet – these guys not yet out of my system! Rly looking
forward, Sx*

'Why?' Bel is close to my shoulder. 'Why are you "enormously enthusiastic"?' I hear an edge. 'I thought you were a writer.'

Is she jealous? So why isn't she photographing me herself? What's happened to this Art Nude project she invited me here for in the first place?

'It's giving me writing ideas.' I hit send. 'It's great he wants to photograph me. I like working with people who are being creative in their own field. It's inspiring.'

'He's got ulterior motives.'

I can't help my horrible self, even though Bel is - I've come to believe - depressed. Suki, queen of the barbed final word: 'Least he *is* motivated.'

A second's silence.

'Right. Whereas I don't think you've even glanced at that unfinished novel of yours yet.'

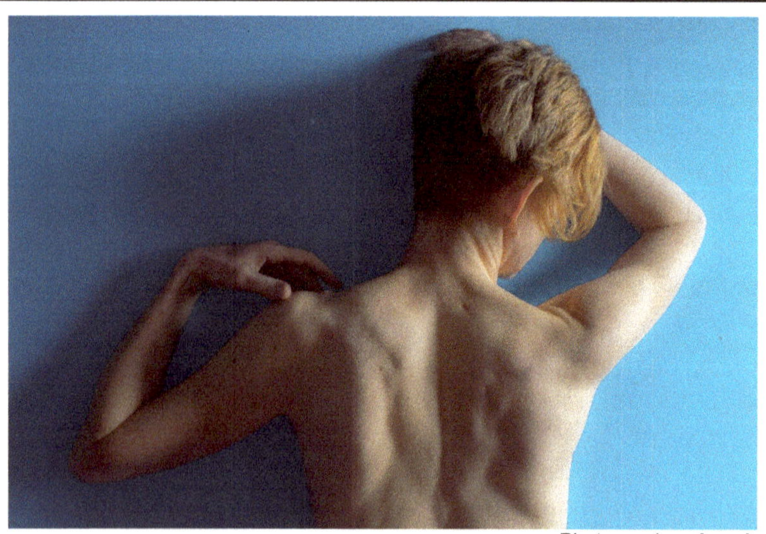

Photographer: **Aussie Cyril**

I feel compelled to modify most of Aussie Cyril's pics. But this is one is great as it is. I love the bright pop-arty blue and rounded corners: vaguely 1960s retro, no?

20th December
Fourth Sunday in Advent

Despite Aussie Cyril's enormous enthusiasm for doing more shoots, weeks pass with no further contact.

It is the fourth Sunday in Advent, and we are hanging out in the flat, not doing much.

Bel is definitely depressed. I realise she's been like this since I got here. Or perhaps, since I've known her.

It's hard not to get depressed when you're living with a depressed person. Should I stay here, in Shanghai? I wish she could bat it away, like we all have to. She scares me. Look, you have to just battle on.

We have free time, the opportunity to do some photography… Should I suggest it? Will I only make her feel worse?

Bel looks up from an email. 'Your Cyril friend. Apparently he went to Australia.'

Darn. I need those lucrative shoots. But I just say, 'Never mind. Guess what - I've just been booked via Wechat by a school-girl for her project!'

Loiza, half-Spanish, a pupil at one of Shanghai's elite European high schools, is the niece of my ex-fling Tamara. She has been given Christmas money by her scheming aunt with instructions to book a session with me immediately (it's her school's Christmas hols)…

…to do Schiele-esque photos 4 my A-level project.
Btw Tamara sent me ur novel & poetry bks – love ur writing –
reviewd Melanie Alone 4 my Eng lit homewk SO ENGLISH – god,
UK gay culture total throw-back -

A new fan! Thanks, Tamara.

Hi Loiza, u r right re throw-back. Novel is set in north, v diff fr
London. Ta 4 praise, if u intrestd, read my autobiog free online at
sukithelifemodel.co.uk. *Lookin frwrd our shoot! c u day afta*
tomoz 3pm Suki x

22nd December
Tuesday

And so, on this ambiently pollution-hazed afternoon three days before Christmas…

'I'm interested in sado-masochism.' Loiza snaps, crouches lower, re-focuses, snaps.

'Ah. Runs in the family, then.' I hitch the black lace she has provided further up above my bony red-stockinged knees. The airy studio that Tamara has financed is, like everywhere in Pudong, brand new, still smelling of fresh paint, minimally furnished other than scattered spotlights, equipment, light-deflecting white umbrellas. Thankfully, white blinds block the views of the financial district's space-age towers that would otherwise give me vertigo.

'Groovy, that's groovy – ' snap snap snap. 'Yeah… When I told Tamara we were doing Schiele at school she posted me the Angela Carter book *'The Sadeian Woman and the Ideology of Pornography'* and that book 'Venus in Furs' by Masoch - have you read them?'

'Can't say I've…'

'She's always encouraging me to be an artist; an experimental, subversive one, though.'

Gurgle, hiss - the electric percolator completes its cycle.

'Espresso break!' Loiza springs over to the kitchen area. 'Here' - she is turning through her school-issue folder of the print-outs of Schiele's sketched figures; the poses I've been carrying out for her. 'Let me read you something… *Charged and explicit eroticism… Near-pornographic intensity… A subversive and challenging vision'* - she looks up. 'That's William Boyd the art critic. Coz like, Schiele did like loads of drawings of himself masturbating? So cool.'

'Um. Yes. Very before his time.'

'Maybe we can get to some of those poses next' - sips espresso - 'You're Tamara's girlfriend, right?'

'Er…'

'Everyone at my school is, like, bisexual, even my Chinese friends. *Especially* my Chinese friends. Straight is just *so* last century. Do you know the photographer Ren Hang? He's *so* cool, you've *got* to check him out. Hey, you sprawled right there holding your cup's great! Wait – [snap] yeah! [snap] Awesome. Can you like, hitch the skirt up further, just like in this picture? So I get more cunt?'

'Schiele-esque' by Tamara's niece Loiza

It is suppertime when I walk into the flat. *'Baozi!'* I hold up the steaming bag of dumplings. 'God, precocious as hell! That scheming Tamara. Got a thousand yuan for it though!'

Bel is standing in the bedroom doorway on her mobile. She quickly finishes, flips closed her phone. 'Sorry. My brother. Did you say a thousand yuan? This Tamara - she obviously likes you...'

The comment hangs in the air. Is she sort of jealous, again? Like her thing against Aussie Cyril?

A flurry: Lily Hong rushing through from the bedroom, a fairy in pink mini-dress, pretty as candy, clutching Bel's iPad.

'Miss Suki' - she's weeping! - 'I reading your stories on internet...' She strokes my upper arm - 'Your baby die. Sorry for you' - squeezes it. 'Too much sad, very sorry.' She turns, hands the iPad to Bel, who has turned to look at me, startled, questioning. Curiously, the back of Lily Hong's dress is fully unzipped. 'Sorry I still here too much long time.' She hurries out.

So I have to explain.

Tuesday suppertime *(continued)*

The bag of still-warm treats for our supper is dangling from my hand. 'I assumed you knew, Bel. I thought word had got round. Sorry.'

'No, I'm sorry.'

'You didn't hear about it from anyone who drew me, then.'

'No. And I didn't keep up with your Two Small Lives[14] serial...'

'Oh god, that! I mean, no-one does...'

'...All along, you must have been thinking I knew. I'm so sorry.'

'...Honestly Bel, I don't expect people to read my story... Just my cathartic online drivel...'

'I did read it faithfully every week, but then... I had a lot going on last winter. I'm just really sorry.'

'No, *I'm* sorry!...'

I go to put the *baozi* on a dish, no longer hungry. I wish I was under my bed-quilt. Alone. I don't want to revisit last year. 'Actually I did email you at the time, but you were... I can't remember now.'

'Sorry, Suki.' Bel is sidling towards the bedroom. Is she, like me, wanting to escape? Are we as bad as each other? 'I had too much to deal with last year,' she says.

'No, it's really alright. It was just, back then, I was thinking you'd be a good person for advice coz we're so similar; like, in age, single, childless and everything. I mean, what would *you* have done if you'd found you were pregnant at forty-seven?'

'I have a daughter.'

'A daughter?'

'Sorry.' She leaves the room.

Why does she never... I need a fag. The rickety screen door to the balcony is permanently shoved back since cool December has seen off the mosquitoes. I go outside, light up.

The way Bel and I relate is so disconnected. Life in Shanghai is, anyway, disconnected. Is that, for Bel, Shanghai's attraction?

The tower-block opposite ours is chequered with murky windows, many now in darkness at this late hour, some still bluish from the depressingly low-wattage utilitarian strip-lights. Millions of people stacked up in functional boxes. At home in England there'll be fairy-lights everywhere, and Christmas trees and candles.

I look down onto the college's ornamental gardens. The staff housing area is well landscaped, albeit in a Disneyland-ish style: ornamental ponds; fake rocks made of something synthetic; a toy-town bamboo bridge. The croak of frogs echoes loudly between the apartment blocks. Bizarre. But nearly lovely, in a way. When all's said and done, it's not desert. It's not Parisian HLMs. It's not bombed-out Baghdad, or an African refugee camp. Why not think positive?

Someone on the paving below hawks and spits. Christ. I can't get used to that. Day and night. The glistening globs make me nauseous. They are everywhere. I tread in them by accident. My skirt trailed into one. They are disgusting.

And we don't know anyone Chinese, and no-one wants to know us. And here in suburban Shanghai there's no bar to go out for a drink. And the internet connection is crap, and anyway it's all censored.

From somewhere above, a dark soft nest comes floating down – the contents of a cleaned hair-brush: black hairs bonded by crud - and wafts onto our balcony, touching the back of my hand. Yeuch.

For all that people are strange and inaccessible, they are much too close.

I put the untouched *baozi* into the fridge and turn off all the lights.

Bel is already in bed with the lamp switched off, thank god.

How old is her daughter? Who, and where, is she?

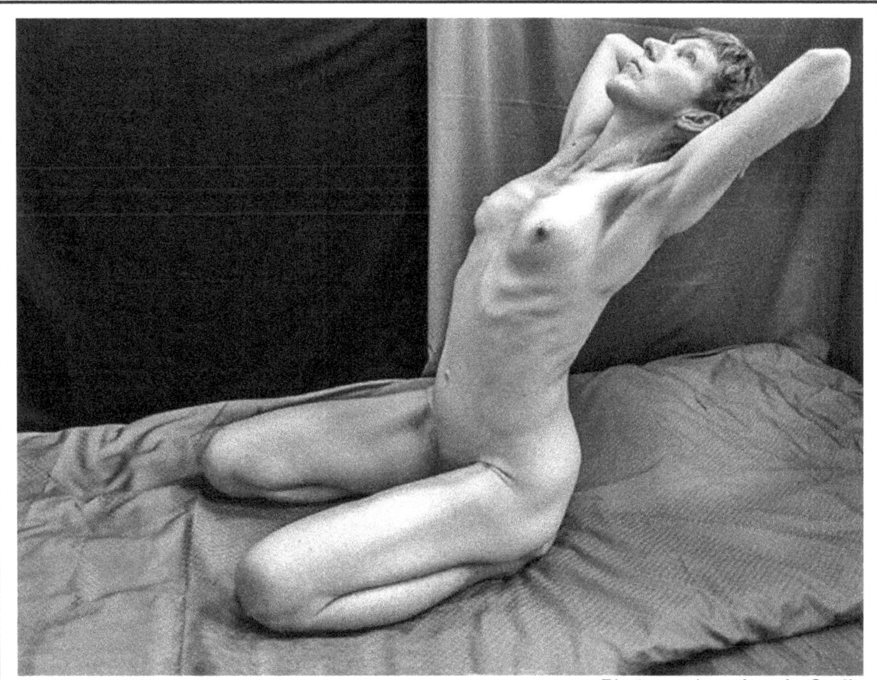

Photographer: **Aussie Cyril**

I cropped and rotated this pic to create the geometry of the black box having its corner exactly at the image's centre, and reduced the colour and contrast to achieve the figure's sculpted look.

PART II

A lonely winter

24th December
Christmas Eve

I wake up. Bel's bed is already empty. Will yesterday's unnerving silence continue? No mention of our respective children? No talking at all, while the elephants move between us in the room?

A text from ex-flingette Tamara!

> *Hey! Wish u cool yuletide. U getting on wid ur writing, u clever*
> *novelist?*

Sigh.

I reach out of bed for my iPad, shoot her an email (cheaper than international texting).

> *No not my manuscript. But readin JG Ballard about Shanghai*
> *wartime anarchy which is makin me write apocalyptic poems -*
> *see attached.*

I doze until – ping! – Tamara replies.

> *Re poem - Shanghai and Bel are clearly bad for your mental health.*
> *I am good for your mental health. You SO need directing. I*
> *would direct you.*

I get up to make tea and find Bel at the window, frowning out at the dirt-heavy sky, an unlit cigarette between her fingers.

'Look' - I show her today's Air Quality Index graph on my iPad - 'bad start to the day.' The red line has steeply risen to "unhealthy". *Everyone may begin to experience health effects, members of sensitive groups may experience more serious health effects. Likelihood of respiratory symptoms and breathing difficulty. Citizens are advised to limit prolonged or heavy exertion outdoors.*

I barely catch Bel's murmur.

'What did you say? "What a thing to have in common"? What thing?'

'The death of a child.'

'What - you too? Your daughter?'

Bel lights her cigarette. 'No - it's just… a dark thought.'

'What is?'

Bel is staring out at nothing. 'And all from a one-night stand.'

Was that little laugh ironic?

Long pause.

I clear my throat. 'I used to be obsessed with wanting to be a mum.'

Silence. That was my useless attempt to prompt. Bel's fingers are trembling. Emotion? What?

She flicks ash. Then - 'I sometimes wish she'd never…'

What?

The rain starts. Little spits. Not enough to wash the filth from the air.

What? *Surely* not…

My voice comes out funny. Like, too low. 'Look, I don't know what to…'

But Bel abruptly steps out onto the balcony, into the rain.

God. How have I ended up living with such a strange person? I don't normally relate this badly. I've got friends, me.

Well, not here in Shanghai, obviously.

I join Bel outside. What a racket! The building-site blasting away. 'Erm. D'you want to talk?'

Drizzle is settling on the grey frizz of her untended hair. Below us, the concocted Disney-esque landscaping; tawdry, on this grey December day. Beyond the campus wall, the incessant soundtrack of construction. Urgent clanking and drilling. On the horizon, scores of cranes that seem to multiply daily.

'A decade ago there was nothing here except swamp.' Bel is lighting another cigarette from her stub. 'And I believe in another decade it'll all be gone again.'

'What – this suburb, or Shanghai?' Pause. 'Or the world?'

'Fake is easier to live with than real.'

Does she mean that positively or negatively? And how can she chain-smoke – isn't the pollution quite enough?

The drilling is horrendous. I zip back indoors. Relief!

I've cropped this to look spiky, Schiele-esque. Not at all suited to the festive season. But this Christmas is looking like a write-off anyway.

Oh how I love my iPad! A couple of jolly Christmassy emails. Tiffany! I'm even grateful for one from the plumber.

But I need to escape further from all this. 'Just popping to the Delightful Peony,' I call out. 'Quick stretch of legs.'

No response.

Hanging on the flat's outside door-handle is – surprise – a gift from Cyril! Back from Australia! When was he at the door? Bel probably wouldn't be happy about this. I shove it in my bag.

In the café I unwrap it. A really interesting book: 'The Lives of the Muses'. Inside is a rambling note.

Merry Christmas to my precious muse!
Please forgive my disappearance. Personal matters in Melbourne
are now decisively dealt with and I am very happy to have ended
that chapter for ever. On to higher things: am curious to hear your
thoughts about Edward Weston to whose photos I'll send you a
link. His muse, Charis, is a subject of this book. Well. my dear Suki,
I have no wish to intrude on the revelries you are undoubtedly
having with your friends. Personally I will be spending Christmas
quietly, alone, in nostalgic reverie rather than revelry. Such is life –
but there is at least a bright star on the horizon who gives me
delight and hope for the future.

I could call Cyril. Now. Get him to whisk me from the Delightful Peony to… to the Peace Hotel, or the Radisson. A rooftop champagne bar…

Aussie Cyril? Yeuch! How can I *even contemplate* that idea for one nano-second?

Because it's bloody Christmas Eve.

Because I am lonely.

'A baby froze to death on the Gaza Strip because it was living under a tarpaulin.' Bel, not long awake, is already frowning into her iPad.

'Oh dear.' I set down at her bedside her morning cup of green tea.

'See! This is why Muslim gunmen shoot randomly into coffee bars. It's simple cause and effect. It's people with no legitimate forum to protest all the historic injustices committed against them.'

'Well, Merry Christmas, anyway'.

She snaps shut her iPad. 'I hate the world, Suki. Where is safe?' -

'Well, let's see...' Oh no - Bel has actually welled up.

'We're all just animals.'

'Look Bel, I think that too. But come on...' I pass her a Chinese rice-bowl overflowing with peanut M&Ms - 'it's Christmas Day.' I watch a tear slide from one eye. 'Sorry they're not Quality Streets.'

Bel throws off her quilt and heads for the bathroom. 'The fact is, "empathy" isn't innate in human nature; that's just a self-righteous myth of Western culture because actually anyone who's non-white and/or non-Christian-heritage is viewed as alien.' I hear her landing on the loo. 'Altruism's a myth too. We only do stuff for others in order to get something.'

'That's fair enough, isn't it, though?' I hover outside the bathroom. 'Like for example, if it's to get love? Hey - are you off out or something?'

'Told you: I'm teaching. It's a normal day. Communist State, remember?' The shower starts but she rants on. 'So-called "values" are purely social constructs created for pragmatic reasons. For particular purposes. Everything's fake. Love is fake. Huh. *Lerv.* I *lerv* ya, babe.'

She is being scarily weird. 'Okay - we'll do gifts later, yeah? And I'll cook!'

Will my cooking lift Bel's mood – or at least distract her? Or be the final straw? I don't know how to help her. After she's gone to work I prepare her an extra gift: a poem I wrote years ago called Bethlehem, after the 2002 Siege of Bethlehem that reduced to ruins the nativity scenes I had learned in childhood. I print it out and decorate its edges.

How to spend the rest of Christmas Day?

I go to the Delightful Peony with my iPad, and email Aussie Cyril.

Happy Christmas Day, Cyril! Am half-way through the book about muses.[15] Edward Weston's photos of Charis are totally about sex. Never mind what this book says - with muses there's always something sexual going on. In Weston's case he has sex with his model at the same time as objectifying the female body to the extreme. The model is no more than a tool. A lifeless plastic sex toy.

As ever, his answer is instantaneous.

Jingle Bells! Hope you're enjoying today as much as our afternoon together yesterday, which has been the highlight of my Christmas. Aha - you think Weston's work is about sex? He always insisted his intentions were purely formal and not in the least erotic. You must have read by now[15] that his nude portraits of the back of Anita Brenner suggest faintly distasteful similarities with his toilet bowl! Yet these are in his own view his 'finest set of nudes… in their approach to aesthetically stimulating form'. *For him they are an* 'absolute aesthetic response... Every sensuous curve of the "human form divine" but minus imperfections'. *Stieglitz himself actually disliked Weston's art nude images, describing them as* "sterilised; …lack[ing] fire, life, [being] more or less dead things not part of today" *(ibid). No sex!*

At teatime Bel returns from class with a polite greetings card from the university's hierarchy and a very pretty box of dried fruits from Lily Hong. Nothing from any students.

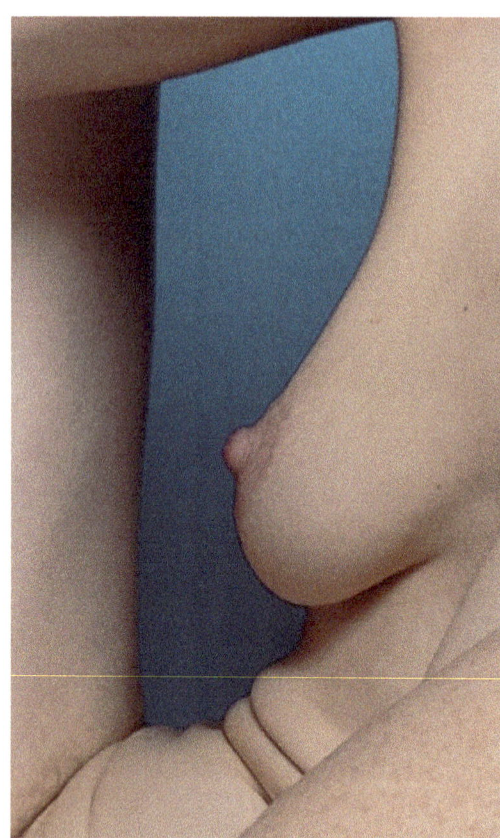

Cyril has lent me an ancient, dog-eared paperback: 'The history of the nude in photography' by Peter Lacey. I'm being educated. Hence, my radical cropping of this image (the uninteresting original being Cyril's) is informed by the hard-edged geometries of Edward Weston who belongs to an important group known as the Photo-Secessionists. In 1902 this group split from the Camera Club of New York to pursue Pictorialism: techniques of manipulating negatives and prints to make them look like drawings, etchings, and oil paintings. They drew inspiration from European art movements with similar goals, such as the Linked Ring. The later works of group member Alfred Stieglitz and those of Weston (who was also influenced by modernists Sheeler and Strand) mark the decisive start of contemporary Art Nude photography. This group did include some women! Clarence White worked with Stieglitz. Also Annie Brigman.

But I certainly don't share Weston's intention to *purposely neutralise the uniqueness of the human form by equating it with inanimate objects*.[15] He took perverse satisfaction from achieving images of the nude that were *'entirely impersonal, lacking in any human interest which might call attention to a living, palpitating body'* (ibid). Is Weston the same type as Uglow? Two haters of humanity?

'Here' - I hand her a Tsingtao beer and clink it with mine. 'Cheers! Let's do gifts!'

Bel opens a small package from Holland: a book on China[16] sent by her brother. Then my poem, and a grey sweater. 'It says cashmere but it might be fake.'

'It's great. Fake's great – it means "authentically Chinese".' She hands me two packages wrapped in red paper. 'For you.'

In a pretence of gayness I rip at them. 'Omigod, where the heck did you find a percolator? You've been trawling those fancy malls!' My second parcel is – 'Oh joy! Thank you so much!' – ground Columbian coffee.

Then she is sidling off onto the balcony. 'Just making a call.'

'Bel – why do you never say "I'm just calling my Mum", or whatever?'

'My brother. I normally call my brother on Christmas Day. Sorry. Excuse me.'

'Got any sisters? Are your parents alive?'

'My brother's it. Childless bachelor, lives in Antwerp because of his solar panels business, very kindly acts as the contact person for Élise. With the unit. He lets me know if he's been informed of anything by the staff. If there's anything to tell.'

'Staff? Unit?'

'Sorry. Élise lives in a psychiatric hospital.' Bel steps outside, tapping at her mobile.

'Oh. Thank you. Sorry.'

Élise. Like *Für Élise.* I guess she might be – what – thirty-ish?

Christmas night. Early to bed. Not a candle lit, not a carol played. Apart from yesterday afternoon (Cyril – overjoyed - treating me to a festive tea at the Peace Hotel), a truly crap Christmas.

Bel is a silent lump in her bed, her lamp already out.

I'll just do one last check for any emailed greetings. And that's when I find it.

One more gift: click on this link.
    http://www.artmartuk.com/blog/a-first-christmas-in-shanghai/
I'm sorry.
Thanks for being here.

1st January
New Year's Day

Bel is let off lessons. The new year begins with us slobbing in bed, luxuriating in Columbian coffee, reading.

'He's definitely after you.' Bel tosses aside a scrap of paper.

'Oh - that my note from Cyril?'

'Just found it by the bed. Do you *like* being considered his "muse"?'

'God no, but he tries to put me in that role by being acquiescent and submissive and just *so-o* over-complimentary.'

'Told you he's into submission. Proper BDSM scene. Collars and chains.'

'Yes. He's sort of hinted at that.'

Bel glances over at me. 'Does that give you "writing ideas"? That why you want to do more shoots with him?' She sounds curious rather than judgemental.

'He *pays* me, Bel. That's the main reason. And secondly, I have free rein to mess about with his mundane photos and turn them into fantastic images. I love that.'

Bel has already drifted back to 'Chinese Whispers',[16] the book her brother sent.

'Great coffee, this! I'll make us another.'

The kitchen stinks of drains. The superficial semblance of a decent fitted kitchen doesn't bear close inspection. Blackened cracks vein the worktops. Door hinges are broken. We put up with the mess of mysterious leaks and dirt traps. It's a mere temporary residence, after all.

Waiting for the coffee to percolate, I receive a call.

A chirpy voice: 'Hello Suki and happy new year to you! Mike Little here. We met at the Shanghai Art Nude Photographers' group about three months ago. Listen - might you be interested in a series of shoots led by my wife Trish who's an artist?'

New Year, new opportunities!

'Hey – brilliant! *Totally* interested!'

A chortle. 'Lovely jubbly. It's her Masters project; something to do with the Swiss semiotician Saussure. I'm just along for the ride. Well: if you can drop by this afternoon for a first 'go', we could make a New Year's Day party of it? Bring Bel along! Long time no see - she hasn't been to the group for months.'

'Wonderful. Don't worry, I'll drag her out.'

'Champion! That'll be grand.'

'Hey - Mike: could Bel be a fly-on-the-wall for this project and make a film recording its progression? Would Trish be up for that? Bel's made some great movies; we can show you some.'

'Sounds magic! Happy days - let's discuss it *anon*.'

When I return to the bedroom with coffee, Bel looks up from her book. 'I'm like Somerset Maugham.'

'Good grief,' I set down the tray, 'why?'

'He felt alienated from the Chinese. Way back in 1900. Just like I do now. Listen to this: *You cannot tell what are the lives of those thousands who surge about you. Upon your own people sympathy and knowledge give you a hold: you can enter into their lives, at least imaginatively… But these [Chinese] are as strange to you as you are to them. You have no clue to their mystery. For their likeness to yourself in so much does not help you; it serves rather to emphasize their difference.*'[16] Bel looks desolate. 'That's me. I have no connection with my students. They don't want to know me. They'd be more interested in me if I had a Gucci handbag. If I *were* a Gucci handbag.'

I thought maybe you liked it that way… A sort of distance from people?'

No comment, but a deep frown on Bel's face, as though examining that thought.

I sigh. 'Never mind - we've just been invited to a party.'

'But don't *you* identify with him, Suki?'

'Look Bel - it's New Year's Day. Think of positives. Plans for this year.'

'Right. So' - Bel snaps shut her book, tosses it aside - 'when are you going to write your novel?'

'When are you finally going to start your Art Nude project with me, Bel?'

'Dunno. It's the teaching. Takes up my headspace.'

'That's not the real issue.' I take Bel by the shoulders and ask, dangerously, 'Why are you *really* here?'

Photographer: **Mike Little**[3]

Mike Little's artist wife Trish draws me on her iPad while nattering on about Saussure's signs and referents and abstraction, then projects the drawings onto my body. Mike photographs the projections. Meanwhile Bel, in fly-on-the-wall mode, is getting material for a movie to document Trish's project. Creative collaboration, or what?

Contrasting to this, the typical relationship of muse to creator is one of acquiescence to the creator's ego. Which is why calling Lee Miller Man Ray's muse is a misnomer, because Lee was simply *using* Man Ray to learn and perfect her own photographic skills. For a classic muse-role of subservience and adulation, see Charis Weston,[17] model and second wife of obnoxious, *'humourless and egotistic'*[15] photographer Edward Weston who picked her up when he was forty-eight and she was only nineteen: *'Charis knew that Weston had a horror of female competition, therefore never touched a camera herself. ...a swooning acolyte who fell at Weston's feet... united with him in a common purpose - his life's work as a photographer...'* (ibid). Bleagh.

'What are *you* really doing here, Suki?'

Holding each other (at arm's length), we laugh. Raucously, theatrically, derangedly: what *is* this life? - ha ha ha… Why have we run away to China ? *Why?...*

2nd January
Saturday

New year, new effort to get to know Bel. Coz we've lived together for more than three months and it's getting stupid.

'Why I *really* came here?' Bel pauses from doing the dishes. 'Okay. I think I came here because if I stay well away from my daughter, no-one can tell me I'm the root cause of her schizophrenia.

'Flipping heck Bel' - I, too, pause from drying up - 'who's been telling you that?'

'It's an established theory.[18] They trot it out.'

'Bastards.'

'Or they don't speak it, you can just feel it in the way they deal with you. As the mother.'

'Who? The doctors? Sure you're not being paranoid? Oh god' - I wince - 'scuse that accidental… Sorry…'

My rapid escape to the Delightful Peony is only for an hour. But by my return, Bel seems deeply under a cloud.

She hands me a substantial tome with the title *Nude: Theory*. 'Your fan just stopped by.'

'What – Aussie Cyril?' (Has the cloud been brought on by the unexpected visitor? Or something else?) 'Why didn't he wait?'

'He just wanted to drop it off.' She is back at her desk, fumbling agitatedly for a cigarette.

'You okay?'

Bel turns to me - 'How can any of us be "okay"?' She smacks at a newly printed-out article. 'Seen this? Climate change is threatening global food supply. Vast tracts of Africa and China are turning into dustbowls on a scale that dwarfs the one that devastated the US in the 1930s...'[19]

I escape to the bedroom, close the door, sit at my makeshift desk. Bel's world scares me beyond words. I need to bury my head in Art, creativity, Adobe Photoshop… Anything to distract myself from the imminent apocalypse.

Dear Cyril,
sorry to have missed you dropping by the flat, thanks for this fab
book! Are you up for doing a proper studio shoot? Maybe at 50 Mo
Gan Shan?? I want to try more Schiele poses. I have props. How
about Monday or Tuesday? Suki x

My dear Suki!
I arrived here at the Delightful Peony a few moments ago, but have
obviously just missed you. If you would permit me to buy you a
rather disgusting sweetened latte I would love to converse with you
face to face? Am sitting here reading about that old goat Picasso's
friendship with Lee Miller. Interesting quote by New York artist
Lee Krasner: the Parisian Surrealists treated their women like
French poodles.[20] You must know that Picasso famously said,
women "make good models and poor artists"? Hope to see you
shortly! Cyril xx

Cyril –
re Picasso: so what. After all, Lee Miller – a liberated, autonomous
woman – was happy to be lifelong friends with him (he painted
portraits of her; she took hundreds of photos of him). There are
plenty of old goats coming out with sexist nonsense all over the
place. They can at the same time be charming and fun and therefore
forgivable. S
PS Soz, can't come to café, Bel unwell.

Dearest Suki,
defend Picasso if you will. This book[20] says that women in his circle
were 'constrained to the traditional art-historic role of a
passive object to be admired, mythologised, dressed and
undressed as the perfect accessory to the male artists'
statement of who they were and how they interpreted their
world.'

His late works depict an ever-lovely young model juxtaposed with Picasso himself looking increasingly decrepit and grotesque. These

images make us "voyeurs of voyeurism", witnessing the artist's desire to possess. Thus we, too, enjoy the fantasy of possession of the "object": the woman.

What is the matter with Bel? Cx

Does Cyril think the way to my heart is to be feminist and right-on? Is that truly, as Bel would have it, his aim? My heart?

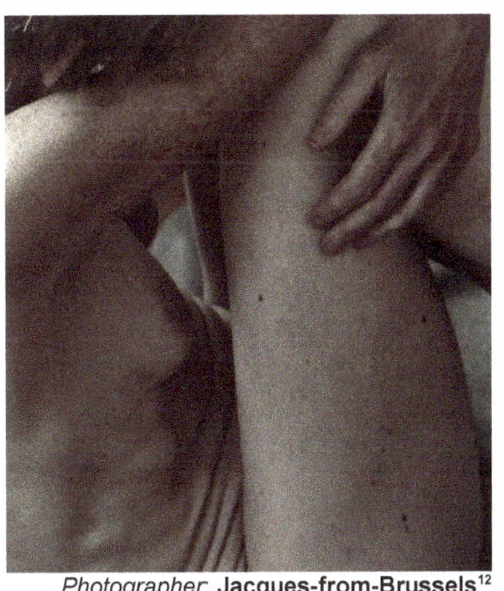

Photographer. **Jacques-from-Brussels**[12]

I've photoshopped more of Jacques' shots from that first group session. Though he is a keen life-long photo-journalist with excellent kit, we just didn't have a rapport. Now that I have cropped this one to emphasise my hideous belly and taken out some colour, intentionally *"making an ugly thing happen"* (to quote Helmut Newton, preceding his emphatic declaration that he "WOULD NEVER DO THAT TO A WOMAN"), I do like this pic. I want Schiele-esque grotesqueness, not Jacques' prettiness.

Yes – not only do I fly in the face of the feminists re Picasso, I also like their anti-hero Helmut Newton! Aussie Cyril's repetition of the hackneyed analysis re: the artist's (Picasso's) desire to possess the object [= woman] is *so* passé. I read somewhere – and I agree – that Picasso's nudes continue, to the end of his life, to represent the epitome of beauty, fertility, and nature itself. Sexist pig maybe, but he LOVED WOMEN.

Cyril –
Picasso's portrayal of an imbalance of power in favour of the male is a reflection of the world he was living in, not his personal misogyny. All relationships are in reality power-games. I think you know what I'm saying. True freedom is when we can choose our roles, and play them out - which we in liberal societies have the privilege to do (unlike in large parts of this world).
Suki

PS Bel is depressed. I'd feel bad leaving her alone, soz.

That's my excuse, anyway.

9th January
Saturday

Good morning Cyril,
have read all the photographers' essays in this book[21] you've lent
me. I like Lucien Clergue best for his prioritisation – even above
setting up the cameras - of his relationship with the model. "Both
the model and I may be completely exhausted at the end of a
session, but it's a good kind of exhaustion". *When*
photographing the model, he is (he says) completely content. Some
of the others in this book - they couldn't give a toss about the model
as a human being.
Can't write more, Bel is just bringing through our elevenses.
Suki

A week has gone by with Bel busy teaching and no proper
conversation. Not my fault. What's the story of her child? How
long has she been in that psychiatric hospital? If Bel had talked,
I'd have talked too.

But now, Saturday morning, over our tea-break, a sudden
change.

'Your turn.' She sets down two cups of English tea on my
desk in the bedroom. 'Why are *you* really here?' She settles on
the bed. 'I mean, it's not all about writing your novel, is it.'

The question is chilling. The January weather, too, is chilly.
Humidity, when the temperature drops and there is no
adequate indoor heater, gets into your very bones. Could I make
Bel happy by saying *I came to Shanghai to be with you*?

But I have to be honest. 'Um. Okay, I'm avoiding my
unsuccessful life.'

Bel reaches over, squeezes my arm (it's always a shock when
we touch): 'Still on your quest,' she says, generously.

'Actually, you know, something's started haunting me – I
mean, being here, with time to reflect: I keep reading articles
about women giving birth at fifty.[22] Ageing first-time mums are
all over the news. If you've got enough money you can make it
happen.'

'God. Materialism *in extremis*.'

'But I'm jealous.'

'Look, Suki. Being a parent can ruin your life. And that's even people like us with all the benefits of living in the West. Wait' – she leaves the room. Is she going to show me something to do with Elise? Photos? But she returns with - oh no - not another article, which she urgently skim-reads, then summarises:

'Listen: tens of millions of poor people in countries like Nigeria, India, Pakistan and Peru can only afford to eat for five days each week. Most of the world is exhausting its ground water because of over-pumping… la la la...' - she skims down - '…yields are flat-lining in Japan... Here! In northern and Western China, and the Sahel region of Africa which is an area wracked by insurgency and conflict, people are running out of land to grow food. Millions of acres the world over are turning into wasteland because of over-farming and over-grazing! It's not just global warming, Suki , it's over-population!'

'It sounds a bit sensationalist, Bel. I wouldn't just take it all as read.'

'This American scientist Lester Brown is saying it, and he's never been wrong about any prediction.'[19]

'Look, just don't worry about big stuff, Bel. Enjoy little stuff. This cup of tea.'

But Bel has dropped back into her default mode.

Sigh. I'm rubbish at dealing with my own depression, never mind hers.

Evening. It is a relief to go out of the flat for the second session at Trish and Mike Little's place. A good distraction for Bel.

Video-camera in hand, she unobtrusively gets to work.

'Is your neck ok?' Mike fusses over me, supervising my positions. 'Are you warm enough? Do you want to sit in that chair? We'll have a cake break in a bit. Happy days!' Then gets on again with his pedantic, conscientious photographing.

Trish bumbles about, switching different spotlights on and off, shifting her projector to create new shapes on my body. 'I've been getting my ideas from this Swiss guy Saussure, who advocated "the detachment of the sign from the referent". Are you with me? It's all ever so difficult...'

'Clever, isn't she,' Mike grins indulgently. He takes another careful photograph. And another. And all the while, Bel - gifted photo-journalist and film-maker *extraordinaire* - sidles around us, doing what she is brilliant at; a silent presence, close to the room's walls, by necessity an outsider, recording it all with her unique eye.

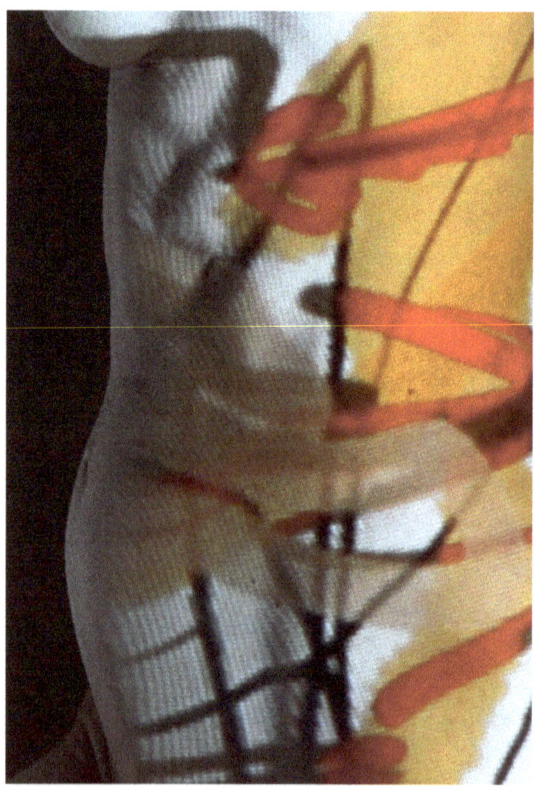

This belly pic is from the second session with Trish who projects her drawings onto me. While Trish worked and rambled on, Bel recorded her voice as well as photographing the process. *'There was this movement among painters away from attempts to paint realistically; you know - figuratively. I think it was due to distrust, because they thought that this kind of "realism" pretended that it knew what the world was like...'*

According to the philosopher-semiotician Saussure (says Trish), the words we use are not a true record of the reality that we are looking at; they are 'motivated signs', and the meaning is *only* within the sign... Etc etc etc

18ᵗʰ January
Monday

The damp mid-January chill of Pudong's underlying swamp-land has seeped up into the apartment block, turning it into a natural refrigerator. Bel has bought two inadequate plug-in radiators – one each for us to crouch over. We are still miserably cold.

Monday morning. Bel trails without enthusiasm to her classroom, and I set out for Shanghai's famous boho art quarter, 50 Mo Gan Shan, a warren of ex-factories and warehouses where Cyril has booked a studio. I expect the shoot to be an icy experience. But it's money.

Just inside the compound, a private photographic gallery has a poster in English advertising a course clearly aimed at ex-pat blokes: *Art Nude Photography: Theory and Praxis*. Judging by the illustrative examples, it's going to be a day of photographing a drop-dead gorgeous nubile Chinese girl's perfect body. In my case they'd have to Photoshop out the varicose veins, the birth-mark, the unruly pubic hair, the mottled knees, the sag-folds, the wrinkles. In fact if I were the model, they'd ask for their money back.

'My dear Suki!'
I squirm out of Cyril's bear-hug. The barren concrete art-space has three small electric heaters dotted around it. Could be worse.
'Here – before we begin the shoot, may I confer you with this warming *quasi* ginger latte - i.e. Chinese version thereof - and I'd like to read you these words by the great Lucien Clergue whom you so admire.'
I sip the synthetic drink. 'I do love Clergue's photos.'
'Well, I think you'll agree that my own *modus operandi* is identical to Clergue's. As he says, you have to be responsive to what the model brings you; models are not objects, they are real people who…'

'Yes - I love that. Whereas so many artists just want a piece of wood. The guys who always wanted to record me like an architect's drawing, why didn't they save themselves the fee and just go draw the bloody town hall?'

'Absolutely! Whereas Clergue says models are "real people who, with a single gesture, can convey a special feeling..."'

'...Brilliant - he sees a model's feelings!'

'As Clergue writes, "These women become my friends and we co-operate in the making of the photographs." I think you'll agree, Suki, that this precisely describes my relations with you...'

Uh? Wait a minute - *definitely* not!

Cyril clearly hasn't noticed the look on my face. He continues, 'Clergue also says he doesn't like working with professional models because the clock-watching interferes with his relationship with them. What are your thoughts about that?'

''He prefers not to pay them?' (Is Cyril intending to convey that he and I now have a "friendship" that makes paying me for shoots inappropriate?) 'Tuh. That puts me off him.' (I must make my position clear!) 'The thing is, Cyril, you and I don't "co-operate". I transform your pictures all by myself with no negotiation. I don't ask for your advice or your opinion.' Callously, I add, 'Nor do I care about your opinion when I'm done.'

'You've created some truly wonderful versions.'

'But even when you don't like what I've done, you never put your foot down.'

'Because I respect you deeply, Suki.'

The more doting Cyril is, the more irritating. 'You always acquiesce. Submit to my ideas.' Oops – that was almost a sneer.

But his eyes twinkle all the more. 'I don't think you know how very fond I am of you.'

Photographer: **Aussie Cyril**

This photo from our very first encounter at the Shanghai Art Nude group looks at first glance like one by Lucien Clergue, 'Deux nus chez Jeff'.

I would feel it a sheer privilege to model for anyone with the skill to glean wondrous imagery from my body, to bring out my essence, my true self... I'd gladly work unpaid for any photographer I was totally wowed by; someone whose images didn't give me the urge to crop or change them in any way.

Who has been that good? Fei Mo Di, for one.

25th January
Monday

Over my shoulder Bel is looking at my iPad. 'One of Cyril's?' She sounds unimpressed.

'Yes - it's from our last shoot. Last week. He was aiming for something like Alfred Stieglitz's 1921 portrait of Georgia O-Keefe's neck. I hate my old woman's face, but the composition and contrasts are interesting. Though I think I've over-photoshopped it…'

'You mean you've gone a whole week without seeing Cyril?'

Was that sarcasm? I don't react to it. 'Yep! Think he's losing his romantic aspirations at last, thank goodness.' (Though I am missing the money).

Ping! A text.

'Ah. Talk of the devil…' I grin (why do I feel sheepish?).

My dearest Suki -
sorry for silence! That fantastic session at 50 Mo Gan Shan last week exhausted me. By the end, sheer concentration was wearing me out. Have needed a period of repose. But we must definitely book that room again. Just been perusing online more of Schiele's work – graphic, sexual. Not surprising that he got arrested for allowing children to see "indecent pictures" in his studio. Have you read anything about his muse Wally Neuzil? Other than Wally his models were always prostitutes. How does one model come to be considered a muse when all others are simply prostitutes? Your Cyril x

Cyril –
Yes please - do book that same M50 space again. Due to that big whitewashed wall at one end, it's perfect for reproducing the Schiele-esque look: sharp, spiky sketches that float without context in blank empty space. Re Schiele's "indecent pictures": the lines between fine art, erotica and pornography are completely arbitrary: culture-bound, generation-bound – don't you agree?

Schiele only drew what he was interested in, especially (it has to be said) genitalia: he would literally just leave some other parts of the anatomy blank, like, he couldn't be bothered to draw the boring bits. But then he was barely out of adolescence when he reached the prime of his career. Don't you find Lucian Freud to be similar? I mean eye-wateringly explicit - serving up his models' genitalia bang in the centre of his paintings like hot dinners on plates. Female models. Male models. His own daughter. I wonder whether Courbet's face-slappingly graphic 'Origin of the World' cunt painting set a precedent, without which Schiele and Freud would never have got away with their stuff?

Btw, I totally agree with art critic William Boyd[23] re Schiele's "superabundant gift" in drawing the human form: "You can't be a truly great painter if you're not an excellent draughtsman" – true, yes? Suki

Dearest Suki,
so much discussion-fodder! May we meet? Dinner at the Radisson tomorrow? An interesting further point in that Boyd article: "Hugely famous and successful artists who draw as well, or as badly, as a 10-year-old are everywhere acclaimed…" Jackson Pollock being one example. What's your opinion on Pollock, Suki - could he draw? And does that matter, especially in regard to the current top popular UK artists? How do you rate Tracey Emin's figure-drawing skills? And David Hockney's drawing skills – is Hockney only good at colour?' Cyril xx

I spoke too soon. He's asking me out on a date. Bugger.

But can I resist the Shanghai Radisson?

After all, I do need to set him straight - *of course* Hockney can draw!!!!!

Why don't Bel and I get into such interesting conversations?

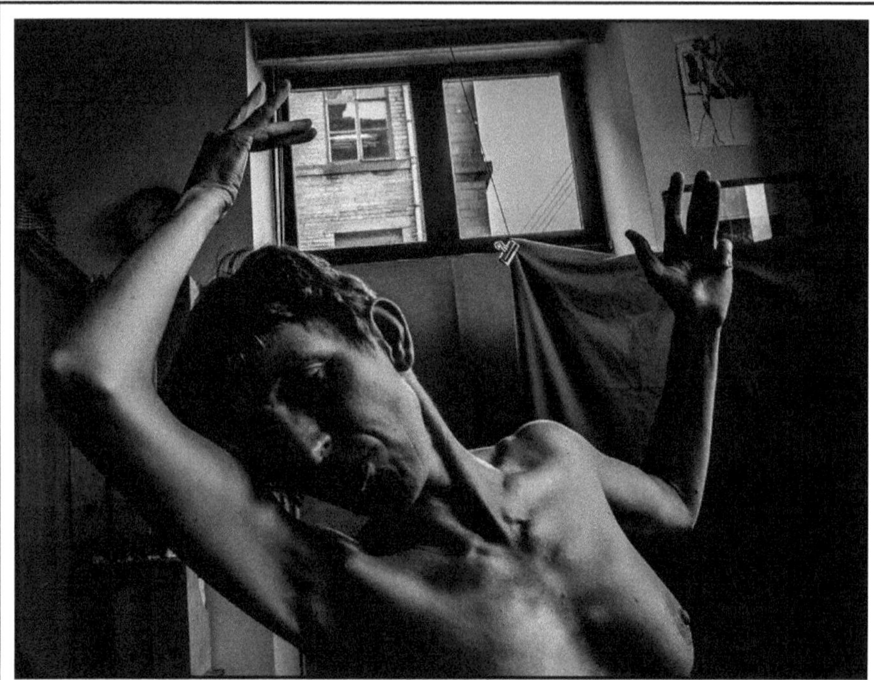

Photographer: **Aussie Cyril**

What's so refreshing about working with photographers is their appreciation of my gestures and movement and personality, in contrast to plodding sketchers whose only mundane goal is "accuracy" – a snobbish aspiration to demonstrate Leonardo-esque drawing skills. Give me any day the photographer-model inter-relationship: an intuitive combining of the flair and spirit of two people.

To be fair, there are artists who *do* capture the moment; artists who stand at arm's length from their easels applying swift, urgent strokes that start from the shoulder rather than the finger-tips; breathless artists with shifting feet who race to produce drawings of a creature on the verge of moving - a model who has flung herself into a wild shape that can only be held for a few moments, her tremulous muscles at snapping-point. Their quick, raw sketches are not about technical accuracy.

But isn't there still an essential difference between artist-model and photographer-model dynamics? I mean, what artist would ever say, *à la* Helmut Newton, "Yeah, give it to me baby"? Note: I'd be okay with Newton saying that because he's so brilliant, but if Aussie Cyril took that tone I'd be grossed out. Also note: on a bipolar scale, Bel is *way* at the opposite end from Newton, ghostly in her lack of assertiveness in the model's domain; silently, unobtrusively documenting the model's chosen way of presenting herself rather than endeavouring to shape the final image. Bel comes at it with *no agenda*.

Is that strange?

Two days since the end of the semester. The students have left *en masse* to spend Spring Festival in their families' fancy apartments in Greater Shanghai or to return to far-flung villages in the provinces. The campus is eerily quiet. So - at last - a chance for us to really talk?

It is freezing. I am under my bed-quilt reading a Guardian article[23] about Schiele and erotica. I turn to Bel. 'Does copying Schiele's and Lucian Freud's poses make me a wannabe porn-star?'

Bel looks up from marking exam papers in her bed. 'No. Why should it? Why should the fact that their paintings are sexually charged automatically associate them with porn? Some of their really famous ones are quite grotesque, not at all beautiful.'

'Yes - that's precisely why I like them. I like edgy; disturbing. It's sex but it's not porn.'

Bel yawns, stretches, seems relaxed. No frowning or agitation. Great!

I warm to my theme. 'Schiele *is* sex. That's why every student in every college class I've ever modelled for is a Schiele devotee. He only drew the body-parts he was into: never mind the head or the feet - straight to the genitals.'

Bel actually grins.

'The only place masturbation's permissible in a school is in the Schiele catalogue in the art room.' *Ping!* 'Oops, excuse me - a text.'

Bel instantly puts her head back into her marking. Darn. I love that we're chatting about Art. That we're *talking.*

'Poo. Cyril. He wants to "*continue our discussion of Picasso*".'

Bel doesn't look up. 'You should go. Get a free meal out.'

'For heaven's sake, Bel, I don't want to socialise with Cyril.'

Bel raises her eyes from the exam papers. 'He never stops asking you for dates, these days.'

'I'd rather discuss Picasso with *you*. I'd rather discuss *anything* with you. Cyril's just... lonely.'

'Go on, then,' she sits back – 'I'm bored of this.'

'Oh! Right - well - Cyril *totally* thinks Picasso's late works are about male sexual power over women. You know – like that Kleinfelder woman's thesis.[4] The fantasy of possession of the model. Whereas *I'm* with this other academic Marie-Laure Bernadac,[24] who describes those works as - quote - "a later-life exploration of the female realm." As in, not exploitative at all.'

'Or at least, not that specifically exploitative,' Bel agrees. 'And anyway, I always wonder what's actually *wrong* with artworks that show a power relationship - a sexual relationship - between male and female?'

'Exactly *my* question! Why is Kleinfelder so derangedly angry with Picasso for relating to women sexually?'

Bel chucks aside her sheaf of exam papers. 'I've never actually understood why artists having sex with models is a problem.'

'Me neither. I mean, which way is the exploitation, in the end? Isn't there a tradition of on-the-face-of-it 'subordinate' female secretaries exploiting their rich bosses for their own ends, by manipulating them with sex?' I get out of bed. 'Cuppa tea?' Heading for the kitchen, I call - 'Traditionally, surely most artists' models would have been expecting it to get sexual?'

I don't hear a response. Please don't stop talking!

I sprint back from switching the kettle on – 'I mean, Schiele's so-called muse Wally Neuzil:[25] she was integral to his life. His primary relationship. Can't we assume it was mutually beneficial? Why insist on calling it exploitation?'

'Maybe.'

'Like, I'm sure Lee Miller fully intended her relationship with Man Ray to be sexual.'

'Well of course, she's a person who would only have sex if she wanted to…' Bel ponders for a moment, 'though anyway she was working more with photographers than artists. I think there might be more likelihood of sex between photographer and model than artist and model, considering that with photography there's much more one-to-one work.'

'I think that's definitely the case. Like, you know Charis Wilson, Edward Weston's 'muse' who became his second wife?

She expected sex with him from the outset. It was Charis who brought it about. Let me get Cyril's book…' I scoot to fetch it from the living room.

Maybe we'll go on being like this from now on? Maybe I could stay on with Bel after all?

Should I get into her bed, to be cozy…?

I dive back into my own bed with the book. 'It says here that the very first time Charis modelled for Edward there was a sexual tension that *"had to be diffused with breathless conversation"* - and the second session, they had full-blown sex which she initiated herself - because he was apparently "shy" - by giving him a *"very compelling look"*. And he goes, *"I felt a response…"'*

We both guffaw. ' *"Eyes don't lie and she wore no mask… At last she lay there below me waiting, holding my eyes with hers."'* Breaking off, I quip cheerfully, 'Bel – is there anything we *don't* agree on?'

'That all men are bastards? Coz you seem very well-disposed towards Cyril.'

Why this sudden barb out of nowhere?

I do another guffaw, a bit over-hearty. '*Obviously* all men are bastards. And Cyril's in the sub-category "fat bastards". Speaking of which, listen to this: throughout Weston's affair with Charis he also kept on a long-suffering and faithful wife in the background who was bringing up his four sons. Quote: *"Poor Flora… I must try to be tender to her, it is not easy to thrust aside such a great love as she offers me".'*

We both go, 'Bastard!'

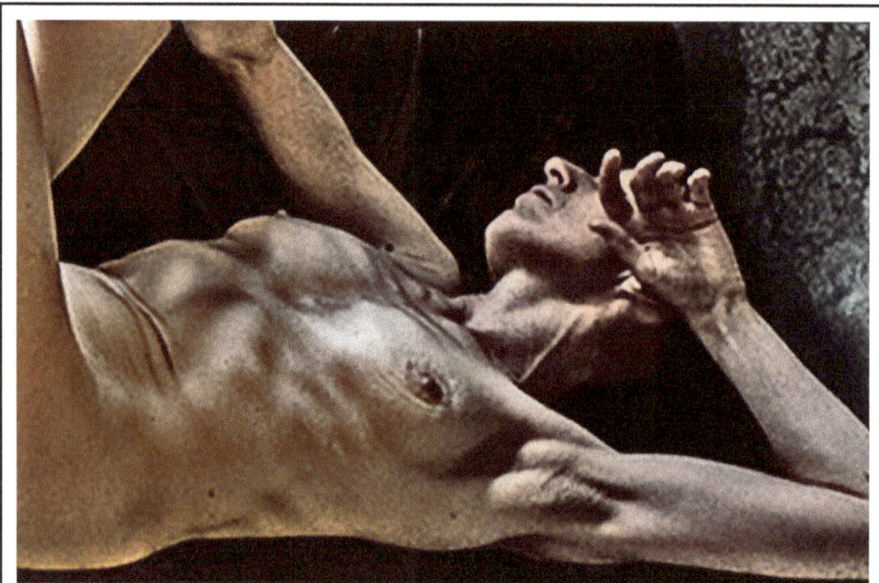

Photographer: Aussie Cyril

At our second M50 session yesterday I got into a pose copied from a Lucian Freud painting. I've probably over-photoshopped it, wanting it to look textured like the painting.

Am I obsessed with Schiele's and Freud's sexually explicit poses? No - just fascinated by the issues they throw up. In an article[23] primarily about Egon Schiele's sexual frankness, critic William Boyd links him with the chronologically much later Freud, whose paintings' *'disturbing power'* have a similar effect to Schiele's notorious explicit nude studies which were a *'visceral shock to pre-First World War viewers'*. The young Schiele - way ahead of his time, and condemned by many as obscene - endeavoured to *'strip away the lies and surface pretences'* 'of social hypocrisy: the repressive values and attitudes that prevailed at the beginning of the 20th century in Vienna and Europe-wide.

Even today, many would be deeply shocked if I, as a life model, copied certain of Schiele's famous poses. I can't think of a single artist acquaintance who would be blasé about drawing me masturbating. Is this evidence of similarly "repressive values and attitudes" even now?

12ᵗʰ February
Friday

We leave the still-empty campus (Spring Festival goes on and on…) to go to the Littles' apartment for Trish's final session. Our suburb is still a ghost-town. The urban population, recently-migrated from the countryside to settle on Shanghai's new-built outskirts, has left *en masse* to return to home villages.

At this annual gathering, do Chinese families fight? Like British families do at Christmas?

With her esoteric art project climaxing, Trish is dizzier than ever:

'…because trying to reproduce an image that you see in a photographic or so-called "realistic" way is about certainty, but there *is* no certainty.'

'As in, nothing can be taken literally?' I clarify.

'That's it!'

'That's how Shanghai makes me feel.'

'We've moved away from the whole of the body' - Trish is pointing at an image on her monitor, 'there - to focus on only a part of the body; hence we've moved from what is obviously a referent, to something which has lost that referent.'

'So you can no longer tell it's anything to do with a body.'

'Exactly.'

'Like these,' pipes Mike, holding out his smart-phone. 'Edward Weston's nude studies. He's in that Francine Prose book[15] about artists and muses.' He shows me a couple of photographs.

'Yes, I've seen some of these. The model's breasts could just as well be seashells or cabbage leaves.'

Mike holds out the phone to his wife. 'This the type of thing you're on about, sweetheart? See - you can hardly tell it's a body. It's abstracted from what it really is.'

'Technically clever – yes.' Bel moves forward into the group from her silent observation-point. 'But the great Stieglitz himself disliked Weston's photography for that reason. It was all about technical prowess but totally devoid of artistic vision. Plus there's no feeling in them. Even though they were often the body of Charis his lover; his so-called "muse".'

'But they're good, though,' Mike insists. 'They fox you into thinking they're something else.'

Behind him, Trish looks pained. 'Haven't you baked something for us, Mike?'

'Sorry Trish, are we ready for tea?' Mike heads for the kitchen.

She sighs and flops in front of her monitor. 'Wish I could talk to someone about my ideas. Wish I was more confident. Always feel I'm waffling, being a nuisance…' She absently drops her mouse into the pocket of her fisherman's smock. 'Most people don't listen to me like you two do.' Is that a comment on Mike? 'Anyway,' Trish yanks at the nest of coffee tables - 'enough of me and my rubbish.'

From beyond the Littles' Ikea curtains comes the constant alien clamour of Shanghai's Jing 'an Temple district. Apart from sharing the ear-plague of incessant fire-crackers, we have no connection with the lives of the Chinese around us at this festival time. Within this apartment, we are in England.

Mike is offering Bel a wide, encouraging grin (she so obviously outside of things; he so patronizingly though well-meaningly trying to draw her in):

'It's quite complex, our little project here, isn't it?' He passes Bel a cup of tea. 'As the photographer I myself am merely observing the primary relationship – which is the artist-model relationship - and recording images of its fruits…'

'But your photos are slanted, Mike. Not objective,' says Bel gravely. 'The photographer's eye inevitably has an interpretative dimension.'

'Accepted!' Mike beams. 'Whereas you, Bel, as a film-maker in this context , are documenting *all* of our inter-relationships completely neutrally.'

'Nothing's ever "neutral",' I pipe up, without forethought - 'I mean, the documenting of my Shibari sessions by a photographer was still shaped by his aesthetic. He was still selecting which shots to take.'

Photographer: **Mike Little**

This photo is of Mike's wife Trish's projection onto my skin of a drawing she did of me on her iPad.

Mike asked me what, in my experience, is different - if anything - about how artists relate to their models, compared to Art Nude photographers and their models.

The fundamental difference has become clear to me. Art Nude photography is dependent on the photographer's personality and his or her connection with an individual model: a photographer can *only* produce Art Nude work if he or she has managed to get into a working relationship with a person who will pose naked one-to-one. Which can be an insurmountable hurdle.

Mike pointed out that Trish's project has been complex, considering there were three individuals making pictures. Yes, interesting. But for me, Trish - as the initiating artist and my director - was my focal relationship. I was not actively concerned with whatever images others present might be trying to capture.

The movie Bel has been making of this unfolding project is almost complete. I am curious.

Mike pauses from reaching floral tea-plates out of a sideboard. 'What's Shibari?'

'Oh. Ah... It's this traditional Japanese type thing... where one gets tied up...'

'Ooh!' Trish's eyes shine, while Mike looks acutely embarrassed.

'It's a kind of meditational practice really,' I bluster. 'The knots have to be really beautifully done. It's more about the process...'

'Bondage!' Trish giggles.

'Uff... Like I said it's very much an aesthetic thing, mainly...'

'How about some bondage, Mike?' She reaches to take the cake-tray from him.

I crash on - '...I mean, the bondage masters are quite nerdy actually, trying to get their knots absolutely perfect and symmetrical and everything' - (Mike is flusteringly removing his pinny) - 'It's more like macramé than anything else.'

'Oh?' his expression changes. 'I used to be really into macramé. Do you remember macramé owls?'

'Oh cripes, yes, macramé owls' – Trish rolls her eyes – 'nineteen-seventies. They were everywhere.' She plonks the tray onto the coffee table. 'Ooh, this looks lovely, sweetheart.'

Mike raises his merry eyebrows at me, then at the lonely island of Bel in an armchair: 'Carrot cake anyone?'

25th February
Thursday

And another week has passed – with the Lantern Festival in it. Another phenomenon we watch from the sidelines – from our balcony – with disengagement; incomprehension. I've looked it up in Wikipedia but… how does it *feel* to those people? Does anyone care? Is it sentimental? Party time? Is it meaningful, or just kitsch for kids? Is it like Hallowe-en? Is it Easter-ish?

And the students are back. And Bel's teaching re-starts. We are back to normal. But what *is* this 'normal'?

I have the latest of Cyril's loaned books – one on Art Nude theory[26] - open in my hand. 'What I like about you is,' I call out, 'comparing you to Helmut Newton doesn't make you go ballistic.'

Bel is in the kitchen tending to a sizzling wok. 'Why should I object?'

I wander into the kitchen. 'My ex Ilka, as a hard-line feminist, was venomous about him coz he says that ideally a nude should give you an erotic feeling.' 'Like, he criticizes Bill Brandt's nudes for not being erotic. What's good about you is, although you think all men are bastards you're still tolerant.'

Bel pushes the tofu around with a spatula. 'To be honest I do find Newton self-contradictory and full of himself.'

'But at least he genuinely likes women! Listen: *"I want a woman who has personality, who is the real thing. She may have a less than perfect body because a perfect form is not interesting by itself. In fact, it is a turn-off. To me, imperfections are much more attractive."* See – he's definitely *not* one of those passionless measuring men. He relates intimately with his models.'

With her fore-arm Bel sweeps hair tendrils from her forehead. 'Intimately. Yes. Like Picasso.'

'I'm fine with Newton shagging his models. At least he wants to *know* them.'

Bel turns off the cooker. 'It's about ready to eat.' I leave the kitchen to go put cutlery on the table.

Bel brings through two steaming plates. 'So what else do you like about me?'

Gulp. I fuss with the condiments, straighten the forks… 'What was that?'

Bel's eyes, when I look up, shiftily catch mine then glance away. 'What else you like about me.' Her tone flat.

'You are absolutely the most *brilliant* thrower-together of strange Chinese ingredients. This looks fantastic.' I ceremoniously take the plates from her hands and set them on their place-mats. '*Voila!* Dinner is served!'

Later, the Delightful Peony provides refuge. And I finally make myself formulate an overdue email to Aussie Cyril, spelling out, at last and in no uncertain terms, the nature and limits of my relationship with him - as I would wish to have it.

Cyril,
I want to make a clear point about our collaboration. As photographer and model we bring together entirely separate skills. Some might believe that the product – the photograph – ought to be entirely the creative domain of the photographer; that the model's part ends with the end of the shoot. Not in my case. Like Lee Miller, I have engaged myself fully with 'post-production' decision-making – as in, making modifications to your original images. While I find certain of your images lovely and perfect, I very often crop the pictures you send me. Radically and with huge enthusiasm. Regardless of whether you might find this an unacceptable adulteration.
I'm being straight with you and I'm sorry if this upsets you. Suki

Oh Suki - absolutely, absolutely not. You are a very strong woman… Presence… I love our collaboration. I feel so proud of giving you something to get enthusiastic about. It's a joy and a privilege to be shown it all as you see it. I think you are a wonderful person and I feel so very, very lucky to have met you and to be involved in this kind of creativity with you. Crop away, dearest Suki. I am always so intrigued to see what you come up with.

Warmest affection
Cyril
PS I am now able to announce - in explanation of my recent disappearance to Australia - that my decree nisi has, at last, come through. Please could you meet with me to celebrate this?

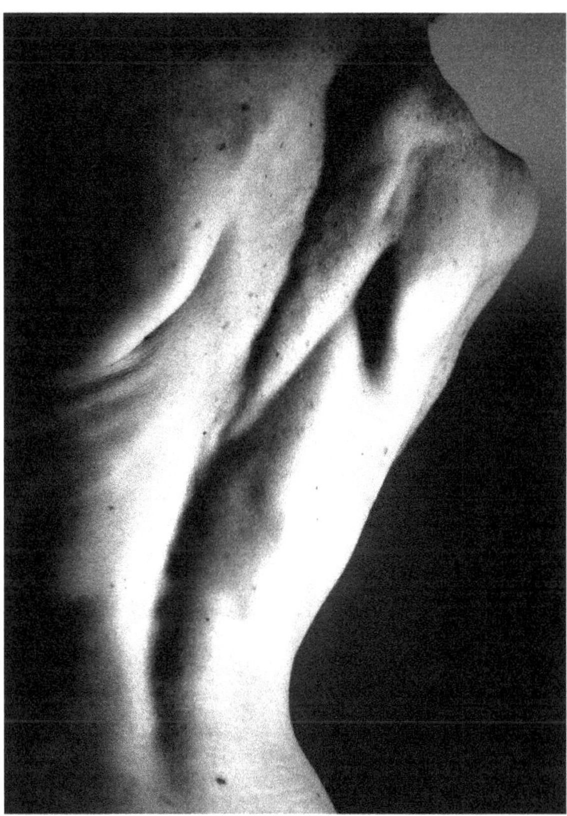

Photographer: **Bel**

Bel's picture of my back reminds me of photographer Helmut Newton's many beautiful backs. He 'adores hard light' because it 'brings out those muscles… The back of a woman shows a tremendous amount of sculpting and modelling'. Although Bel's 'back' photos are not in Newton's brilliantly light-drenched Californian settings, they do make me look sculpted. Newton states that 'naturalness' is not necessarily what he wants. This provokes the ire of some feminists - or purists, perhaps - who hold 'naturalness' to be kind of morally favourable. Whereas Newton claims models themselves often choose to put their bodies into positions that are not 'natural', and that anyway, manipulation just gets more interesting results.

I insist in the face of all controversy that I like Newton. I like him for being especially interested in the female body and finding it so much more aesthetic than the male body. I like his immediacy, abrasiveness, spontaneity - and unashamed voyeurism! *'The trouble with a very controlled nude is that it is not voyeuristic any more.'* [26]

29th February
Monday

The Air Quality Index has leapt in the night to 'hazardous'. By the end of this afternoon's teaching Bel is wheezing so dramatically that she gives up the ghost on our planned attendance of the internationally-publicised (by Mike) 'private view' of Trish Little's final exhibition for her MA in Fine Art at the Cohan Gallery. We are not entirely sure what Mike "consults" about, but he's got a finger in the pie of a dozen embassies and has invited VIPs galore.

The main constituent of the event is a big-screen premiere of Bel's movie,[27] with its sound-track of Schubert interspersed with Trish's breathless commentary, subtitled of course in Chinese.

An inevitable text from Aussie Cyril:

May I drive you ladies to the Grand Event this evening?

No worries Cyril we already have a lift. Maybe c u there

Darn. How to avoid him?
I take the Metro, and arrive late: the end of the first screening. The gallery is off a leafy lane in the French Concession. Omigod: embassy staff; entrepreneur types - penguin-suited ex-pat men and their shrill women in glitzy, plunging gowns.
I find Fei Mo Di near the champagne. 'Thank god. Look – protect me from Aussie Cyril will you?'
'Darling,' He kisses my cheek - 'it will be my honour and delight to have the model of this performance-piece on my arm for the evening. Where's Bel?'
'Nearly dead of pollution; she can't breathe.'
'Oh lord! Frightful!'
I take a canapé from the tray offered by a Chinese hostess in red silk dress. 'No expense spared!'
'The subtitles are crap,' sniffs Fei Mo Di. 'Mike had them done by an agency. Got ripped off. He should have asked me.'

'So what - it's not about the subtitles! Who cares about the subtitles?'

'Oh, I know that,' Fei Mo Di turns to me with his champagne. 'Please congratulate Bel for me. She is a superb film-maker. Everyone's completely bowled over. Did you hear the British Consul waxing lyrical? Come on – I'll introduce you.'

I am late back. Bel is in bed, ashen-faced, gloomy.

'You're famous. *Really* famous. I mean, among Shanghai expats. *Time Out* was there. And the *Shanghai Daily*.' I hand her a bottle of champagne and give her a kiss on the cheek. 'Now, or tomorrow?'

She looks at me. Then at the champagne on the bedside table. What is she feeling?

'Tomorrow,' she wheezes. 'After I finish teaching tomorrow. It'd be wasted on me now.'

I can't go to bed yet. Too much excitement. So I end up emailing Aussie Cyril my latest transformations of his pics. Knowing that there will be not the smallest squeak of opposition.

Cyril -
attached are further radical crops of your photographs. I am frankly proud of them. I bet no model's input in the finalisation of the image has ever been this extensive – not even Lee Miller's participation in Man Ray's work. But since you have assured me that I have free rein, I am continuing to make new pictures from your pictures. My decision-making, my agenda. The agenda of the personality in charge of the image at the point of the photo being taken is all but obliterated. Not collaboration. Domination. S

There'll be no objections. It's what he gets off on.

A minute later, I get an email back...

Suki my darling,

you were absolutely lovely in every sense this evening; I am so sorry that you got whisked away before I could see you home myself. Regarding these pictures, there is not a ghost of a chance that I will ever take offence at your creativity with any of my images. I will even send you via Dropbox the TIFF versions, thus you will have more scope for your modifications. Collage, montage, abstraction - I am fine with anything, everything.

May I reassure you further - over dinner tomorrow night?
All my love,
Cyril xx

While I'm still reading this, ping! A text from Cyril on my phone!

Please come outside. I am at the east gate of your campus in my car. Sorry it is rather late but I have something very important I wish to say to you.

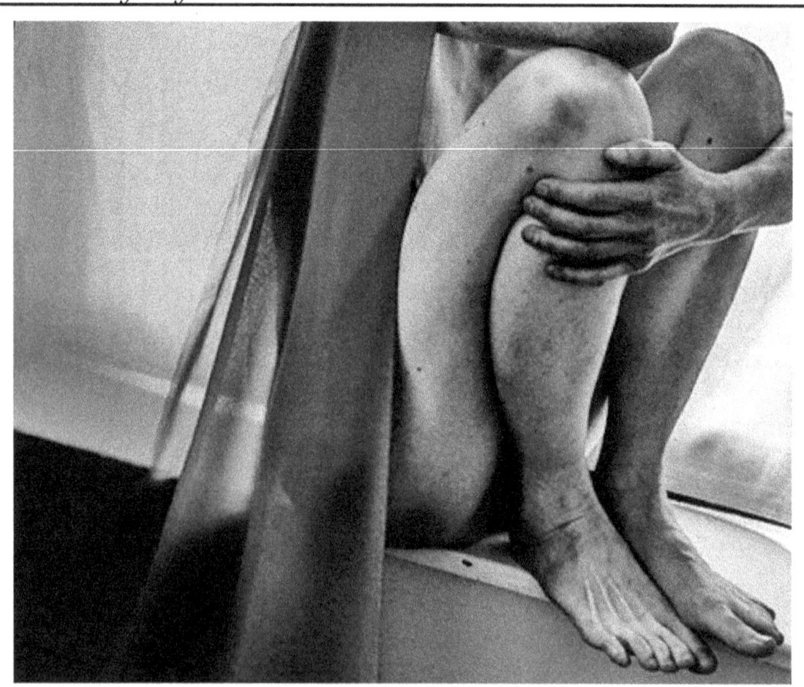

Photographer: **Aussie Cyril**

I continue with zeal to radically modify Cyril's photos, in view of his wimpish lack of protest - thus transforming them from (in my opinion) bland to amazing. This one now looks slightly solarised, in the style of Lee Miller and Man Ray.

1ˢᵗ March
Tuesday

The Air Quality Index has only slightly improved: *'unhealthy for sensitive groups'*.

'Morning! How are you feeling?'

Bel coughs hard. Rubs her eyes. 'Lily Hong said the air's going to be [splutter] better in March.'

'Good! Here - thought you'd prefer tea first, before the champers.' I set down the cup at her bedside. My head is full of last night's incident, of which I cannot speak.

'Thanks, but the champers'll have to wait til I knock off.'

When I awaken my laptop I find among the morning's freshly-arrived emails – bugger – one from Cyril, which I quickly skim:

...how wonderful every day would be, to be witness to that heady combination of your enthusiasm, creativity, and joie de vivre... As said, ...so much materially to offer you... little me...
Your servant,
Lots of love, Cyril

Hey - there's also one from Tamara's photographer pal, Hong Kong Ron! Recently arrived Shanghai, wants to photograph another Shibari session, Tamara has put him onto a master rigger, am I available this week?

Bel, creakily sitting up in bed, glances over, then searches my face. 'What's up?'

'Uff,' I half turn – 'nothing up. Just another booking for this week. All good.' I hesitate. 'To be honest, I've got a bit of a Situation.'

'Oh?'

'Cyril's asked me to marry him.'

'Told you.'

'Actually it was late last night when I went out for that fag. Sorry. I've been in shock till now.'

Bel flings herself out of bed - 'I always said "ulterior motive"' - and slams into the bathroom. Is she that upset?

'As you know, I find him physically repulsive,' I call through the door.

'There'd be plenty of advantages,' she calls back. Crash – 'Ow! Shit.'

Advantages? Having to dominate Cyril? *I* want to be the subordinate one. Told what to do. I want someone to take over my stupid life and govern it better than I do. But not Cyril!

There is no more talk. Bel slams off to her class.

Later I email Hong Kong Ron back, fix up a session for tomorrow night in the Bondage Master's apartment. For an evening I will gratefully be guided, led, controlled, instructed. All I have to do is obey. Submission is so uncomplicated. And furthermore, highly valued. It's a good bargain for both sides.

Late afternoon. The Delightful Peony's one heater breaks down, so I return to the flat to hunch over my little radiator with a fistful of new poems. Apocalyptic imaginings: a tsunami obliterating Pudong, the Jin Mao Tower collapsing due to the sub-standard concrete of its construction, the Peace Hotel bombed and in flames. I get two plastic tumblers ready for Bel's return. The champagne is chilling in the fridge.

A call from Lily Hong. 'Miss Suki, please come. Bel's daughter is died.'

'What? Pardon?'

'Bel is here. In office. Please come.'

In the Foreign Affairs office I find Lily Hong seated in front of her computer screen weeping, together with Bel, around whose shoulder an arm is draped.The screen is filled with a China Airways webpage in Chinese.

When I walk in, Lily Hong nuzzles at Bel then relinquishes her chair for me.

Bel is impassive. 'I'm booking a flight, but not for straight away. My brother can deal with it all.'

'What happened?' Fearful, I reach, lightly touch her cheek. 'How did you hear?'

Her face twitches away. 'John called' – she looks at her watch – 'about an hour ago.'

'How..?'

'Oh, she just died.' Pause. 'About 11pm Holland time. Heart failure. People like Elise are full of anti-psychotic drugs and massively overweight. And she chain-smoked.'

I do what Lily Hong was doing. Bel's shoulders under my arm are wooden, unyielding. She seems tight-coiled, ultra-controlled.

'I'd rather miss the funeral and everything.' She scrolls through dates. 'Let's try for a ticket in three weeks.' She looks up at Lily Hong. 'I can buy this ticket now with my credit card, can I?' Then, like an after-thought, 'Maybe I don't even need to go.'

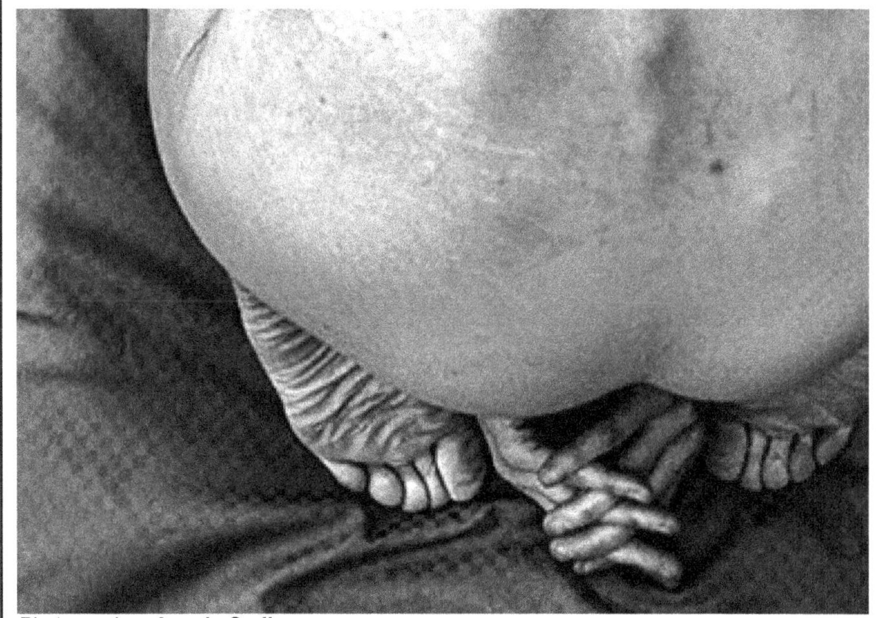

Photographer: **Aussie Cyril**

Cyril's photo. My radical crop.

PART III

The countdown

4th March
Friday afternoon

The pollution has soared even since this morning. *Very unhealthy: increased aggravation of heart and lung disease and heightened risk of premature mortality in people with cardiopulmonary disease and the elderly. Reduced exercise tolerance in people with heart disease due to increased cardiovascular symptoms such as chest pain.*

You can be solitary without being lonely. But you can be lonely even when you are with another person.
    Searingly so.
    I think I'd learnt that by the age of about ten.

I'm at the window when Bel walks in, coughing hard, from her afternoon class.
    [*Splutter*] 'What are you doing?'
    'Thinking. Nothing. Look at that filthy air.' I don't say – *One year ago today I gave birth.*
    'The students say Shanghai's no way as bad as Beijing.' Bel drops her briefcase and immediately goes through to lie on her bed.
    Today is technically Bel's third day of mourning. Two dead children are in the apartment with us. We are being intensely silent with each other. Has she nothing to tell about her daughter? Or is it that she can't say it?
Today is also exactly five months since the start of my life in Shanghai with this impenetrable, unhappy woman who is wracked by ever more terrible coughing fits.
    I continue to stare, unseeing, out of the window. How can I possibly stay here? I can't speak the language. There is no outlet for my work here. I can't do poetry readings. I can't share poetry. And internet censorship blocks out my world. What has Shanghai done for me? What, actually, am I?

    "I'm a writer and poet. Yes - I'm published."

"Actually I'm an art-nude photographic model. I know - I look quite old for that! But I've got other strings to my bow, for example Shibari bondage… Oh, and I write."

"Me? I'm just a sad old tart."

Being a sad old tart, should I grab Cyril's marriage proposal and exchange exhilarating, dangerous, unstable, polluted, desolate Shanghai (and Bel) for his native Melbourne?

Aussie Cyril, or Bel? Edifying conversations about Art, or depressing daily bulletins about the end of the world?

Would Cyril want me to whip him and lead him about by a chain? But might the material benefits amply compensate for having to do this – e.g. is Cyril rich enough to buy me a baby? Could he make me an ageing first-time mum?

Cyril versus Bel. God. Rock and a hard place. Unless - might Bel change? Get happy? Could we ever get… close?

Sigh. What other options do I have?

I deliver a cup of tea to Bel wheezing asthmatically in her bed. I want to talk about our children. There are two elephants in the room. But Bel is closed off, scowling into her iPad.

So I sit at my desk, check my inbox.

One new email. Tamara.

Hi – just got Hong Kong Ron's fantastic photos from Wednesday's session. Guy I booked to do rigging tip-top! Learned his craft in Japan. Check out Japanese photographer Nobuyoshi Araki - pics of incapacitated women. Intended to empower women. Not depictions of a woman but of his relationship with her. His aim is, free women's souls by tying up their bodies.
Soz for long silence my end, Dad getting poorly.

Tamara is so bloody brilliant at making things happen for me. Or should I say - *to* me. Is returning to Blighty and crashing indefinitely at her designer apartment my best option?

But…

The thing about marriage is, it's SECURE. No financial worries, ever again. Secure, secure… When was I *ever*?

Bel emerges from the toilet. Over my shoulder she spots an Araki image. 'You still into bondage?'

Does this mean she's up for talking? 'Yes. It fascinates me.'

'Oh, but it's not 'real'; it's just stylised enactments of power roles. Being tied up is both aesthetic and symbolic…'

Bel has gone to poke among her stacked-up books. 'I bet you don't know that Lee Miller did sub-dom role-play with Man Ray.' She starts leafing through the biography.[28]

An opportunity: I say, 'I've been thinking about Lee Miller. D'you think she was - um - inured to death?' -(clever - managing to bring up the 'd'-word!) - 'Like, didn't feel anything about it?'

'No.' Bel's book snaps shut, and her face, too. 'Why?'

'Well, she seemed so unfeeling. Even before she saw all the blood and guts in the war.'

'I don't know what you mean.'

'Well, for example, why wasn't she affected by the suicide of her fellow-model, the beautiful Nimet - considering she may well have played a role? I mean, it happened soon after Lee started shagging Nimet's husband, the old Egyptian guy - which was pretty treacherous of Lee, especially when she'd photographed Nimet herself, which shows they definitely knew each other socially. Could it have been to do with the rape when Lee was seven? Childhood trauma? Like, she learned to just blank people out? No empathy?'

But Bel's phone is ringing. She checks it, mouths brother, and goes out onto the balcony.

I stare down at the biography. Should I just give up on trying to live with Bel?

What on this earth induced me to come to Shanghai? If I'd known there'd be days like today - our apartment nightmarishly patrolled by two ghost children…

If someone would only take the reins of my stupid life out of my hands, I would submit to their every wish.

Photographer: **Hong Kong Ron**

I love the textures in this shot. Two days ago I slipped away to the session with a Shanghainese Shibari bondage master arranged by Tamara's photographer pal, Hong Kong Ron who, it turns out, has not just randomly popped up again in Shanghai. Tamara paid his flight - as well as a fee. And the rigger's fee.

Who said anything about sleazy? Ultra-classy Lee Miller and Man Ray were into domination and submission. In about 1933 they were spotted in Montparnasse connected by a gold chain. Though from what I know of Lee Miller, she'd have been rubbish at being subordinate. *'The woman was taller than the man and strode along in spite of being tethered.'*[28] The observer commented it was obvious the man was more attached to the woman than she to him.

7th March
Monday

Bel is later back from teaching than usual. I've been happily awaiting her return because I've got a suggestion. It might get her out of herself. It might kick-start her Art Nude project with me.

'How was your morning?'

Bel drops her briefcase. 'Crap.' She undoes her coat but doesn't take it off, and flicks on the heater beside her desk. It is mid-March, noticeably warmer with spring round the corner. 'You seem to feel permanently chilly these days, Bel.' I set down a tray laden with tea and Shanghai-style custard tarts. 'Listen: do you want to make another life-room movie?'

'I can't. I've just been booking a flight to Antwerp. Lily Hong helped me.'

'Oh!' (God, can I survive here by myself?) - 'I thought you'd decided there was no reason to go back.'

'My brother's insisting. There's bureaucracy to deal with. I fly on the 25th of March and come back after two weeks.'

'Two weeks?' (Phew, I can survive that) - 'Well, this life-room thing's tomorrow night at Qi Qi's Café-bar in the French Concession. It's some designer friends of Fei Mo Di. It's an actual life-drawing session.'

'Okay. Yes. I'll do it.' A slight, albeit wan, smile - 'There's two weekends before I fly when I can work on it. Should be able to get it finished.'

'Brilliant! Hey – you could try and get some shots of me to start the ball rolling for our Art Nude project when you get back!'

'Will you still be here when I get back, Suki?'

Gulp. 'Why wouldn't I be?' I feel a blush of shame.

'You've got options. Do what you want.'

'You need Lily Hong more than me. To survive here. I'm rubbish at helping you…'

'Not true!' Pause. 'But I only want you to stay with me if it's right for you.'

'I don't know what's right for me, Bel.'

Uncomfortable silence. Then - 'If I were never to return, you'd *have* to decide something.' She wanders off to the kitchen. Obviously a rhetorical musing that I don't need to answer. Phew.

Afternoon. I head out – keep to my usual weekday routine, even though on Mondays Bel knocks off earlier. I need to leave her behind; her silence. But ten minutes after my arrival at the Delightful Peony the power goes off. With no heating or lights, the café is miserable. I quickly finish my latte and scurry home.

The whine of the neighbour's erhu is floating down from the upstairs flat as I let myself in. I urgently need to pee. The bathroom door is off the bedroom, so I storm on through. The quilt on Bel's bed is puffed up high, covering the single trunk-shape of Bel and Lily Hong. Their twin heads look conjoined on the one pillow; their bodies must similarly be pressed close.

'Sorry!' I slam the bathroom door, yank at clothing, crash onto the loo. I understand it. Warmth. Comfort. I don't know whether they've taken off their clothes. Is it sex too? It is silent out there. I bustle back through the bedroom without looking and scuttle to the kitchen. Then I pick up my iPad and go for a walk. Give them privacy.

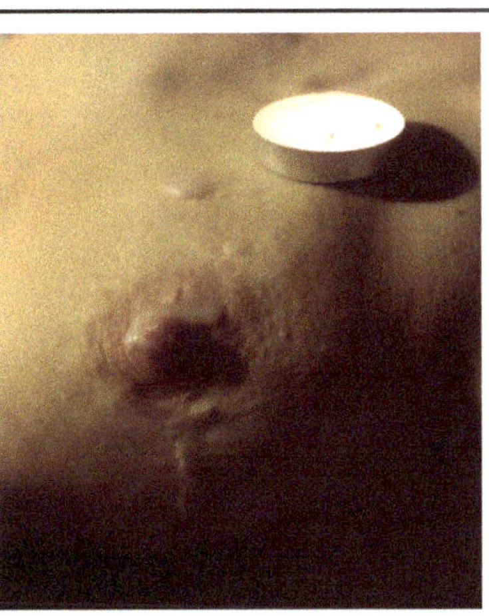

Photographer: Hong Kong Ron

Another pic from that bondage session a few days ago. There are other physical experiences one can submit to. This one was my idea. It didn't hurt. What I get off on is giving someone my absolute trust.

I settle on a lonely bench on campus, near enough to the library to get a weak-ish signal. I've received a new email with photos attached. Sent at 04:00 UK time.

Hi – just quickie - Hong Kong Ron emaild me another batch of fab pics fr that last session. Not only bondage. They did good work wid u. Followd my instructions 2 letter. Am in hospital waitin rm. Tamara

'Control freak' is barely sufficient to describe Tamara's megalomaniacal omnipotence. I like being controlled.
I feel comforted.

8th March
Tuesday evening

Air Quality 'moderate': *Unusually sensitive individuals may experience respiratory symptoms and should consider limiting prolonged outdoor exertion.*

A slight reprieve for Bel.

On our taxi journey to the life-drawing session at Qi Qi's, Bel mentions, 'Lily Hong will be meeting us there with a voice-recorder to get some vox-pops for the sound-track.'

'Brilliant!'

Hesitation. Then - 'she confides in me.'

Is this an oblique reference to their *triste* or whatever it was yesterday? 'Good! That's good.'

'She's lonely, is Lily Hong.'

After twenty minutes of warm-ups the group decides they want one long pose for the rest of the two hours. And thus I am able to retreat peacefully inside my head in a way that I used to do every day in my former existence, modelling for artists. Without knowing it, I have missed this. Swimming thoughts become ordered.

On the long Metro journey into the city Bel had shown me a really interesting homily on the Guardian Online's book pages,[29] warning today's parents against telling children they can be whatever they want – because it is so difficult to achieve those big dreams, to reach for the stars and attain them – barring a lottery win or some fluke of good fortune.

This novelist, Tim Lott, says that, given the competitive nature of modern society, it's better to keep our enthusiasms and passions for our hobbies. He claims he has gained the most joy in his life through the commonplace activities of home, family and hobbies, rather than his actual profession. The latter, despite having given him a few particular moments of success and reward, has taken a high toll in terms of effort and struggle and disappointment.

It's better (he says) to ask children not *what* they want to be, but *who* they want to be. The capitalist regime benefits from us all believing that it is purely success in the workplace that makes us a success as a person. But we are presented with only two alternatives: superstardom or – that loaded term – mediocrity. As such we are all – almost all of us – going to endlessly feel disappointed in ourselves and our achievements.

It's good, what he's written.

Shouldn't I aim to be, first and foremost, a kind, generous-spirited person, rather than a writer?

Throughout the session, lovely Qi Qi keeps asking, 'You okay? Enough warm?'

'I'm totally happy thanks!'

But I'm not totally happy. Why can't I be content with my modest successes - my small online readership,[30] my poetry collections,[31] my novel, my collaborative movies[32] with Bel, my prowess as a doughty energetic model? I already have a legacy to leave to this world. Is it time to just stop questing, stop striving, think small, local, intimate; stop getting on aeroplanes, try settling? Is it time to commit? And thus reap small, satisfying benefits? I am approaching my half-century of life. Is it time to give something back, rather than fret that I haven't received enough?

I don't even notice Bel's camera clicking away. She's so cleverly unobtrusive. It's wonderful to be working together again on a small good thing.

It's late when we get back to the flat. I bring Bel hot milk in bed. 'It'll already be a little bit spring-like when you get to Antwerp!'

But she has lapsed back. Face closed. Remote. Incommunicado. A terrible state that is more and more her usual one.

How could she not have been uplifted by this evening?

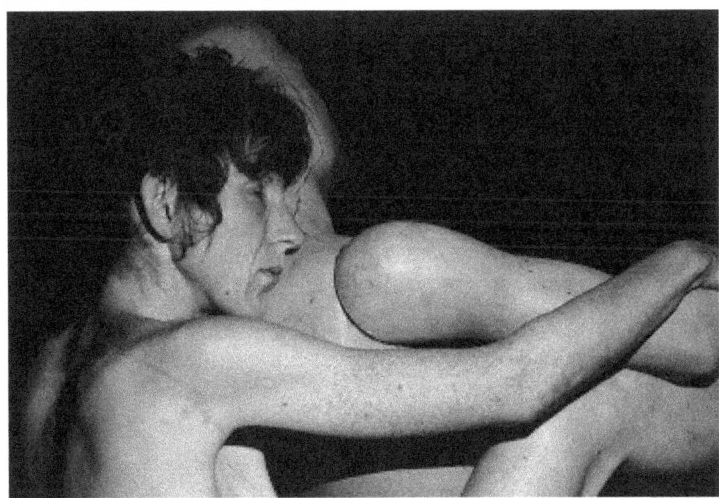

Photographer: **Greg-I'm-a-Kiwi**[33]

Interesting props were provided by Fei Mo Di's friend Greg-I'm-a-Kiwi for today's life-drawing session at Qi Qi's boho café-bar.

10th March
Thursday

My 'alarm clock' (Bel's hacking cough) goes off early today, but she manages to settle back into dozing.

So I have got up well before her; left her rattling under her duvet. As I'm putting on my coat I call, 'Make sure you get a chest x-ray in Antwerp.' I pop back into to the bedroom, looking for my hat.

Bel rouses her head. 'More creativity with Cyril, this morning?' Did that wheeze have a cynical tone?

Look, I don't want his pictures any more. I'm doing this purely for the money.' I stare at her. 'You look grey, Bel. I'm phoning the office for you. Don't go to work. You can't breathe.'

I set out for M50 - my third shoot there with Cyril. On the Metro I become terrified. What if I arrive home to find Bel dead in her bed? An asthma attack. Heart failure. A strain of pneumonia that brings instant death.

Alone in Shanghai… God. I would die too.

But she answers my text.

Ok tanx. Hav good morning.

At the studio Aussie Cyril's ten-day-old marriage proposal hangs in the air, brings an intimacy (- uncomfortable, unwanted), like ten days into an engagement.

I don't refer to it. Maybe it will sink away, be forgotten…

'Over to you, Cyril. You choose the poses.'

Or should I do something about it? At least they would understand my poetry in Melbourne…

'Thank you, Suki. Today I'm aiming to reproduce the classical nude portraiture styles of Henry Callaghan or Ruth Bernhard; also a fashion photographer who turned to Art Nude called

Jean-Loup Sieff, who took *"lively portraits of interesting girls"*, to quote the excellent paperback I've lent you by Lacey'.[33]

'Girl? I'm not exactly a spring chicken.'

In the evening I receive an email with his "classical nude portraits" attached.

My dearest Suki-muse,
permit me to inform you about the gentlemen who have been my influences. Emmanuel Sougez's figurative female nudes attend to composition, line and form, though the individual femininity of his models is not subordinate to these concerns. Harry Callaghan on the other hand creates images which represent the model's nature or character (yes, a stark contrast to Edward Weston), bringing out femininity and modesty coupled with a psychological remoteness and elusiveness. Women are his chosen subject: feminine, demure women "like mythical beings" who are revered and turned into fantasy.[30] While Callaghan's pictures are not remotely pornographic – he maintains a distance and respect – his way of relating to the image of woman is nothing if not sexual.
By the way, did I ever say, I love those images in which your eyes twinkle? Cyril x

I rattle off -

As so often, you are again trying to make something pretty of me. I don't mind not being pretty. I'd rather not be. 'Callaghan-esque' is a style I really don't like. I'm not a mythical being. I am not remote.

But I must not sound so churlish. Cyril is still paying me. So I delete this, and write -

Thank you Cyril.
These are beautiful. I love looking at beautiful women. I am not one. But they are lovely. Thank you. Look forward to more sessions. Do suggest a date. Suki

Clearly Cyril is hovering somewhere, awaiting my responses. I immediately receive his reply:

Dear Suki, my darling muse, how about another shoot on Monday morning, first thing? Then lunch at the Peace Hotel? Let me know.

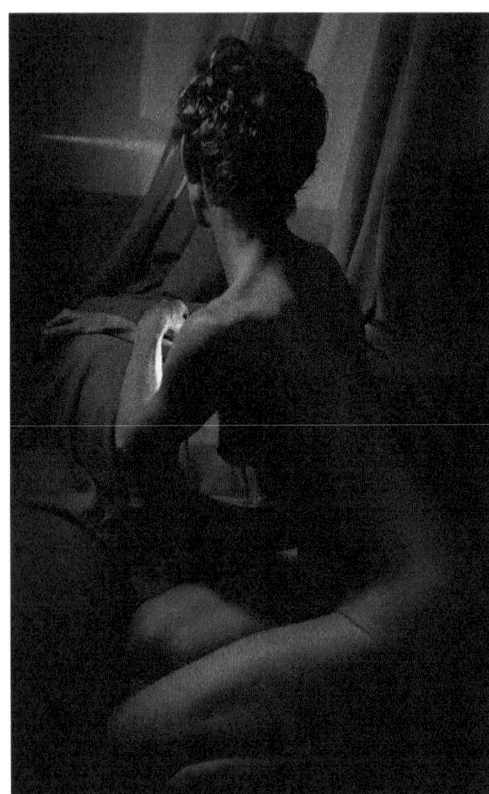

Cyril's photo is in the style of Emmanuel Sougez's 1930s nudes, which "are meant to be sexually admired, but... represent the old-fashioned discreet view of women; an ideal of femininity reminiscent of 18th century artists Fragonard and Boucher ...*purely and simply feminine ...seeming to shrink before our admiring gaze*"[30]. Yuk.

I continue to transform Cyril's originals to create an entirely different end-product. He has turned his latest black and white ones soft and gentle, but I have brought up instead a stark contrast. The bottom line is, I have fundamentally different aims from his. I emphasise geometry, shapes, contrast.

I now keep my cropped versions of Cyril's and other people's work in an 'Art Nude' folder of my own. I no longer want to share these with him. They are *my* creations. Mine.

11th March
Friday afternoon

I'm in the Delightful Peony.

It no longer matters that the café's heater doesn't work: the temperature these days, with spring coming, is ambient. Shrubs in the roadside-landscaping are beginning to blossom.

Another email from Cyril.

Darling Suki-muse! Ferenc Berko "turned to the nude for her beauty and challenge".[30] What do you think? Another romantic, like me? Cxxx

It's started to feel like an 'online courtship'. *Bleagh.*

On the plus side, it's the only conversation I get.

Dear Cyril, re Berko: that's interesting because life-drawers similarly talk about 'challenge' – yet are coy about, or actually deny, looking for beauty. And what, anyway, is 'beautiful'? "The curve of the neck, the turn of an ankle", comments artist Helen Wheatley[35] in Bel's docu-movie 'Under the gaze'[36] (watch it online – it's brilliant). Berko seems to emphasise the torso. He shows very few faces. And uses lighting and textures to create a mood. Yes – he is definitely another romantic. Not realistic.

What I think? Yuk - give me realism and grotesquery any day. Sorry to disappoint. S

Evening.

In her non-teaching time Bel has dived into making the movie about Qi Qi's life-drawing session as though there's no tomorrow – though there's another fortnight til her flight to Holland.

But tonight, with the weekend ahead… Perhaps there'll be the odd window for a conversation?

I deliver another cup of tea to her desk.

Bel pulls out her ear-phones. 'The sound-track's great, though I say so myself. Got any biscuits?'

A smiley face! And her breathing seems easy. 'Of course it's great. You're brilliant. I'll fetch the Oreos.'

Bel stretches in her seat. 'It's mostly Maria Callas singing an aria – Qi Qi's choice. But we'll need subtitles for these vox-pops I've edited in. I can't ask Lily Hong, her English is too poor. Who can we get to do it for free?'

'Fei Mo Di is the obvious person. He's the only person I've met who's totally bilingual. I could offer in exchange another one-to-one shoot for free. I'll go message him.'

By the time I return from texting in the kitchen (better reception at the kitchen window), Bel is pacing, scowling at a dog-eared A4 sheet in her hand. 'I've just re-found this article. It's really scary, Suki.'

(Deep sigh) - 'What?' - I hold out the biscuit tin. How can her mood have changed so suddenly?

She ignores the biscuits. 'Global demand for food is outstripping supply because of climate change. In some parts of China villagers are abandoning the countryside because the land is too depleted to raise flocks or grow food. It's even starting in Japan. This American scientist Lester Brown[37] says it's all coming to a head - and he's never been wrong in any of his predictions.'

'Don't you want an Oreo?' - Ping! - 'Yey, a text from Fei Mo Di! Let's see…'

Yes, am up for this skills exchange, curious re Bel movie, wd like to support. Yes can do subtls tomoz, come my place in morn afta 11, do shoot first then lunch then work?

'Listen, Suki: there's already millions and millions of people in poor countries who can only afford to eat five days a week – even actual water is running out because of over-pumping. In northern and western China, and somewhere in Africa people are running out of land to grow food.'

'God, Bel. Give yourself a break.'

'It's all going to collapse. I watched the Twin Towers live on TV as they collapsed. All this. Here in Shanghai. It could all come tumbling down in a minute.'

She so frightens me.

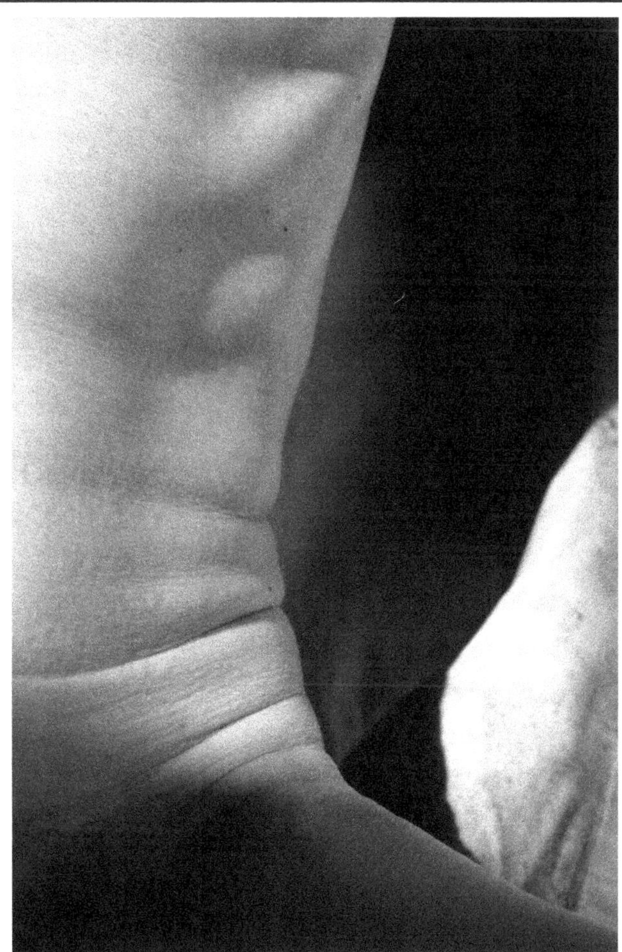

Photographer: **Bel**

One of Bel's pics from Tuesday's fly-on-the-wall documenting of the session at Qi Qi's café-bar. I suggest she modifies it to give the body a more radical outline like Man Ray's and Lee Miller's solarisation. It could even be made to look like Ferenc Berko's experiments, which were unique in his time ('sixties) - images that looked like sketches, nearly abstract. But Bel ignores my advice. She is no Cyril.

12th March
Saturday afternoon

'My German boyfriend walked out on me last October after seven years.'

Seems Fei Mo Di had other motives for our 'skills exchange' arrangement. He's needed a shoulder to cry on.

'Seven years! I split with my German girlfriend after *seventeen* years.'

Being the self-obsessed type he doesn't pick up on this. 'He said I was too British. Emotionally stilted.'

'That's rich, coming from a German.'

'At Eton I was too Chinese.'

'Is there a place to live on this planet where you don't get stereotyped?'

We both have a think. I come up with - 'Alone in a lighthouse on a rock off the coast of Scotland.'

Fei Mo Di looks morose. 'I wouldn't get a visa.'

We are drinking pastis in the after-lunch peacefulness of the *Café des Stagieres* on Yong Kang Lu. Our conversation meanders and our solidarity builds while we slave over the subtitles for Bel's movie.

A new pal. An afternoon of happiness.

And then I am back in the flat. Bel working on the movie; me staring at my emails. At some point I make Bel a mug of tea, place it by her elbow, squeeze her shoulder. *Wish you could be happy.*

It's as though she hears that thought. 'I don't think I could settle back in the UK, Suki.'

I sit down beside her. 'Why not?'

'I feel alien there. Did I ever show you what JG Ballard wrote about the English when he first arrived in England after the war?[38] After he'd grown up in Shanghai?'

'No. but I guess it's not an uplifting read.'

'He influenced me to come here. Although he was describing how things were in 1946, so much of what he wrote is still true.'

'Like what?'

'Oh… narrow English attitudes; English greyness; English misery…'

A brooding pause.

'You know, since all my international travelling, my photo-journalism work, I've felt utterly alienated from England. The culture, the politics…' She trails off.

'It wasn't only to escape from your daughter then. Coming here.'

'Not really. It was mainly coz I got this job offer and thought – why not? Good as anywhere. And JG Ballard had made me curious.'

'But we're alien *here*, too.'

Bel turns even more glum. 'True. When JG Ballard was here he lived in a privileged and comfortable ex-pat bubble. Today's equivalent of that in Shanghai is repulsive and I avoid it.'

'Tell you what.' I push her shoulder gently. 'Let's go live in a lighthouse on a rock off the coast of Scotland.'

'What?'

'Drink your tea.'

And since then until now - late in the night – we've been immersed in our respective silences; our separate virtual worlds.

Cyril – your original version of the attached portrait embarrassed me: I had an expression like a parrot. I wish you'd acknowledge that apart from when I do a big smile, I am not photogenic. Don't patronise me with the pretence that I am anything other than interestingly ugly. A "straight" portrait photo of me is a non-starter. There are millions of photos of amazingly gorgeous women's faces out there in the world. I refuse to be entered into that competition as the booby prize candidate. Anyway - the way I've now cropped it, it's primarily about the hand, though the face is still discernible even though I've cut off half of it.

But Cyril's response is, as ever, dotingly acquiescent.
  Tsk.

Photographer: **Aussie Cyril**

Cyril's shot. My excellent crop.

13ᵗʰ March
Sunday morning

The BBC is blocked today. They must have done something to wazz off the Chinese government. My VPN isn't working either. Routed out and blocked.

I hate it. I hate not having free internet access. I hate living in a totalitarian state.

So when am I going to leave?

What if – terrifying thought – Bel were not to come back from Antwerp?

She's spent this whole weekend til now beavering on the 'Qi Qi's life-room' movie. Silent. Shutting me out. But it's better than obsessing over the world's bad news, I suppose. She's still got to put the subtitles on, but I'm sure she'll get it done. There's another weekend before she flies.

'Just off to my shoot with Cyril!' I want as many fistfuls of yuan as I can get out of Cyril. I'm jittery about my cash-flow during the time Bel will be away.

'Good morning, darling Suki-muse.' Cyril hands me my usual ginger latte from the downstairs Starbucks.

But I am cross. 'Don't, Cyril. Muse is *not* the word. It's as bad as saying Lee Miller was Man Ray's 'muse': it positions her behind him, like, in a purely supportive role, when actually it was Lee who invented that famous 'solarisation' technique.'

'Alright. I'll call you my darling *directrice*.'

'Tsk. Stop it. Look, the facts are, (a) Lee spent at the very most three years with Man Ray, and (b) she used that relatively brief relationship as an apprenticeship to further her *own*, not his, photographic career.'

'All I mean is, you inspire me. Give me something to do. Without you, I don't really have… here in Shanghai…'

God I don't want to hear this - 'Cyril! Listen - a proper muse is someone like Charis Weston; it was her *raison d'etre* to further the work of her photographer husband. Like, it was her sacred obligation. Whereas I do *not* further your work, Cyril. I chop it up and make it mine. Muse is *not* the word for me. It's your silly fantasy.'

He pats my bottom. 'Deary me – which side of the bed did you get out of this morning?'

Why am I risking upsetting him with honesty? He is paying me more than the going rate. Pretence works for both of us.

'Sorry Cyril. Let's just get on with the shoot.'

Allowing the bottom-pat is just necessity. But I decline his lunch invitation.

So I'm back at the flat in time to have lunch with Bel, which for once I myself cook. Maybe we'll talk! Though I've given up prompting Bel on the subjects of her daughter, her past, herself…

I prepare instant noodles with flare, serve Bel at the table with a flourish, and embark on an interesting topic.

'Bel. I have a question. Art Nude photographers, even female photographers, mainly take pictures of women. Whether exploitative or reverential, it's always women. Why?'

Carefully, as though teaching a little child: 'Because women are more beautiful.' Then, with chopsticks midway to her mouth – 'Well, except for Robert Mapplethorpe and his gay stuff, obviously.'

I coil my noodles round a fork. 'Okay, so I have another question: why don't men – straight men - make themselves beautiful? It's not as though they don't get looked at, in this day and age. Why don't they feel themselves being looked at, and get self-conscious and worried like we do? I mean - Aussie Cyril's obese. Mike Little wears a zip-up fleece and socks and sandals, need I say more. Jacques-from-Brussels clearly never bathes. Hong Kong Ron, that friend of my friend Tamara – he's a buttockless little shrimp in unflattering spectacles.' I scoop at the noodles' greyish soup. 'There's only Fei Mo Di who looks good.'

'Obviously. He's a French horn.'

'But the rest of them - they make me want to holler *Hey* - you men - it's the twenty-first century and people are looking at you!...'

'*I'm* not.'

'...They should get their peacock tails out! They should make themselves more attractive! Just make a bloody effort, guys.'

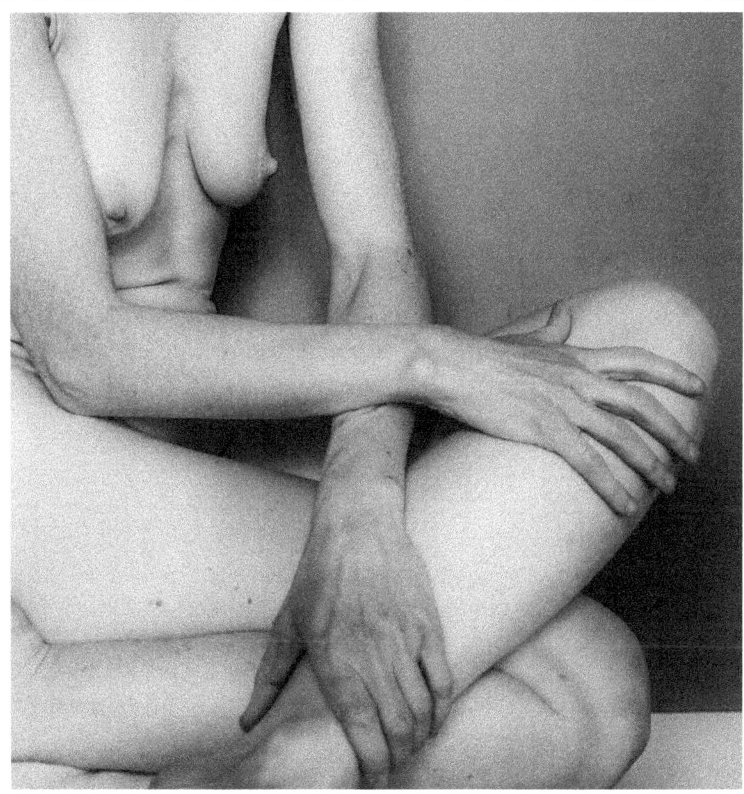

Photographer: **Aussie Cyril**

Cyril says the work of Ruth Bernhard inspired this photo. He pointed me to Bernhard's 'mission statement' (summarised in Peter Lacey's book[34]): *every artist is a missionary trying to convey a message of truth and beauty; further, the immortalization of the human body's beauty – both male and female – has always been an obsession for poets, sculptors, painters and now photographers. However, in her twentieth century context, the image of woman is being cheapened and exploited – especially by photography. Thus Bernhard saw it as her life's task "to raise, to elevate, to endorse with timeless reverence the image of woman".* Cyril seems entirely at ease with Bernhard's quasi-religious attitudes. Cyril, too, has a similar reverence for women. Tuh. His photos from the latest shoot *still* aim to beautify me.

20th March
Sunday

It's been a weird week. We're both being weird. Carrying on as though this is an ordinary, normal, uneventful life with no pain in it.

I head for the Delightful Peony, leaving Bel obsessively fine-tuning her movie, something about matching the images better to the sound-track…

I might as well be in a remote lighthouse as here in Shanghai. I feel like all my bonds are cut with my past. Where are all the people I had in my life up until last year? Well – call it nine months ago, when I left England.

What's Tiffany up to?

What about Ilka in Berlin?

I even wonder occasionally about single-mindedly ambitious Conservative Bastard Jeremy (he who didn't want our child). But only in abstract terms. Because he is a man of physical beauty. He's probably painting the queen by now.

What induced me to leave it all behind?

Why suddenly up and leave a life?

Only Tamara has kept in regular touch. What does that say?

When I walk in later, Bel, still at her desk, thrusts her iPad at me while remaining focused on her laptop. 'Read that. It's warped.'

The iPad shows a page on the Shanghai 'Meet-Up' website - the profile of a newly-founded group:

'Elite Social' new exclusive Meet-up Group for informal networking at cocktail parties and fine dining events in Shanghai! Guests will make valuable contacts while socialising and networking with many quality professionals at prestige venues. Membership not open like other Meet-up Groups, 'Elite Social' is private club, monitors all applications and approve only people are stylish, successful, like-minded professionals, appreciate finer thing in life. Average age mid 20's - mid 30's, various nationalities. All member need have photo. No fake profile. Welcome to

'Yeuch. Imagine the combination of Western jerks and oriental princesses.'

Bel pauses from typing. 'Totally. It epitomises the Shanghai we get pulled into as westerners,' she growls. 'It's why I've never socialised with the international community. When you're working in Afghanistan, the Balkans, Africa, it's totally different. I hate how people relate here; especially the encounter between foreigners and this privileged social stratum of Chinese.'

I consider my almost total lack of relations with the Chinese population amidst which I've lived for a half-year. There's only been Fei Mo Di – but he's an old Etonian; Hong Kong Ron - but he's Hong Kong-ese; Lily Hong.

'When is a favour not a favour?' Bel is grimly wiping today's layer of smut from her monitor. 'When is a genuine compliment a fake compliment? When is an act of kindness not an act of kindness? When is a friendship not a friendship? When is a smile fake? Who can be trusted – if anyone?'

'Um. Well, Lily Hong, obviously. Aren't you being a bit extreme?'

'Tuh.'

'What?'

'Lily just wants a passport.'

'Not fair. She's your good friend, Bel.'

Silence.

I reach, touch Bel's cheek, but this unnervingly transforms her scowl into a desperate, searching look. I just blunder on - 'You do need to leave Shanghai. Not just for two weeks – for good. You're being poisoned.'

Midnight.

Bel comes to bed at last. 'Done it.'

'Hey - fantastic!' I sit up. 'That's fantastic.'

'It's not that good. ' She starts to undress. 'Just alright.'

'Rubbish. I know it's brilliant. Look - let's have a launch party before you fly off on Friday! I can put out word on the SANP WeChat group; Mike Little will rally folk.'

'No!'

'Why not?'

'I absolutely don't want a party. I don't want to meet people. I hate people. Everyone out to get something from each other. Nobody being straightforward. Nobody being genuine. Only being nice coz they want connections, favours, advantages.'

'But… why put all this work into this wonderful movie if you don't want to show it to people?'

'I needed to kill the time. You know; get completely absorbed in a task. Before the funeral.'

'Funeral? I thought you'd intentionally missed the funeral…?'

Sigh. 'That was my hope.'

'…thought that's why you decided not to fly straight there when you first got the news...'

'It was. But there was a delay for the post mortem, then another stupid wait for a cremation date. Bloody bureaucracy,' she stares out of the window. 'Funeral's the day after I arrive.'

Photographer: **Aussie Cyril**

This started as Cyril's; now it's mine. I worked on the colour and cropped off my head, but the thing that 'makes' it is that I rotated it until I got the sense of suspension. I am very pleased with it.

21st March
Monday morning

Air Quality Index: Hazardous. Serious aggravation of heart or lung disease; premature mortality in people with cardiopulmonary disease and the elderly. Severe respiratory symptoms such as wheezing and shortness of breath in people with asthma; aggravation of other lung diseases. Increasingly severe respiratory effects likely in the general population. Impairment of strenuous activities and serious risk of respiratory effects in general population.

'Bel, you cannot go to work in this filthy air. I'm phoning Lily Hong to say you're sick again. They can cancel your classes – half the students won't show up in this, anyway.'

After phoning, I take Bel's breakfast to her bedside. Ominously her nose is already stuck in her iPad.

'Oh dear.'

'Listen to this - the novelist Yu Hua[39] summing up modern China: *"So intense is the competition and so unbearable the pressure that, for many Chinese, survival is like war itself. In this environment the strong prey on the weak, people enrich themselves through brute force and deception, and the meek and humble suffer while the bold and scrupulous flourish"'*.

'This country is upsetting your equilibrium. Here. Drink your tea. Maybe you shouldn't come back after all, when you're done in Antwerp.'

The look on Bel's face chills me. 'Joke!' I plonk myself on her bed. 'Don't you dare not come back! What the heck will I do? They'd throw me out on the street in a minute. I'd be living in one of those migrant workers' temporary huts…'

Bel coughs hard, then looks grave. 'The truth is – the truth that's *denied* by the capitalists is - there's no such thing as a level playing field.'

'Look, Bel - maybe you should watch a nice movie or something. Reading the news is bad for your health.'

'In a minute. Listen – this article by Pankaj Mishra[40] is so important, about how capitalism developed and how we are responsible for it. We British, I mean. It fits exactly with what JG Ballard said.[38] Mishra says the belief systems and institutions we initiated - like, the global market economy and stuff - caused the big fuck-up of Europe and this is what's now also fucking up Asia and Africa. It's like, there's no alternative any more. Socialism finally died a quarter of a century ago, and since then this capitalist paradigm of desire and consumption has spread right across the globe.' She looks up at me from her iPad. 'Why the big sigh?'

'It's just all too much, Bel.' I sip my tea (evil British colonialist Typhoo).

'But this is *so important.* Capitalism *relies on* everyone believing in the level playing field, when in truth it's purely and inhumanly a machinery for economic growth, or in other words, the enrichment of the few. Listen: *since 1989, the "neo-liberal fantasy of individualism" whereby talent, education and hard work are rewarded by individual mobility, has proliferated and spread worldwide, even as structural inequality has become ever more deeply entrenched…'* It's what's wrong in China…'

'Look. We can't do anything about this. Why get so upset?'

Bel plows on: '…The American illusion of equality of conditions which says "anyone can make it if they try" spreads false hope. Plus, it promotes being an entrepreneur to a higher status than any other occupation.'

'Everyone in Shanghai *is* an entrepreneur!'

Not true! Not those guys out there right now digging up that tree;' Bel points out of the window, 'those migrant workers from the countryside who live in those prefab huts. That's China. People like them.'

'So do you think there'll be a revolution? Or is an apocalyptic catastrophe due to climate change the more likely thing to hit Shanghai first?'

'Social unrest. It'll start with social unrest. The trouble is, people's sense of their own powerlessness and deprivation is much worse today because everyone, everywhere, including poor people, has tellies and mobile phones where they can see other people's wonderful lives. Resentment builds up because we can constantly compare our crap lives with the lives of the wealthy and privileged...' She suddenly looks hard at my skinny wrist. 'You need to eat. You're really scrawny.'

At last I've distracted her from politics!

But Bel never comments on how I look. She's *seen* me! What does this mean?

Cyril's photo. My crop, my adjustments. My body. My creation.

21st March
Monday morning

Two days before Bel's flight.

Ought she to be grief-stricken? And ought I to be empathetically distressed, reminded of my own tragic loss of a child? Why aren't we clinging to each other?

I'm scared.

She has taken to wearing her anti-pollution mask even indoors. I think it's partly about privacy. Like doing a long pose. A retreat inside yourself. Or behind – literally – a mask.

It's not just the air that's been poisoning Bel. Something in the atmosphere of this alien land is polluting her mind with dark thoughts, nightmare scenarios, apocalyptic visions. She's made me feel afraid too. A sense of foreboding. A creeping anxiety. Are her fears irrational?

'Bel - I think it's good your contract finishes at the end of this semester. It forces a decision about moving on. For both of us.'

No comment.

I turn to finishing off a thank-you email to Fei Mo Di for the photos he sent from our "skills exchange" session.

... my amateurish, unskilled, gauche behaviour when being photographed. Having read descriptions of the actual process of Helmut Newton's shoots with his models, and seen his contact sheets and the amount of trial and error, i.e. how long it took to get the one shot where the model was - at last - doing the 'right' thing that 'made' the photo, I feel a bit better about my own shortcomings as a photographic model. But I have come to realise and appreciate how patient you have been.
Love Suki x

Bel's laptop is emitting a gentle Chopin nocturne.[41] Above her mask her eyes are on the colour-adjustment tool in Photoshop, very slowly sliding the cursor along the spectrum. When she speaks the mask puffs in and out. Like a surgical mask. A brain surgeon asking to be handed the next sterile tool.

'What?'

Again she wuffles, 'do you love me?'

I clamp down on panic.

Bel pulls off her mask, remains studiously focused on her monitor

Have I made Bel love me? Have I misled her by coming to Shanghai? And does that make me – oh god – responsible for her? For her unhappiness?

Do I love Bel? What does that *mean*? How do I feel?

I don't need to conscientiously examine my feelings because instinct is instantaneous and honest.

I care about you. But I don't fancy you.

I say, 'You know what Prince Charles said when Lady Di assured reporters upon their engagement that they were "in love"? He goes "Whatever that means…"'

Bel's dead, unmoving stare remains on her monitor.

I reach and give her shoulder a swift squeeze. 'I mean, what does "I love you" mean?' I do a sunny grin. 'You're amazing. I'll make us a cup of tea.'

The Delightful Peony beckons. The incessant mournful whine of the erhu in the upstairs flat is the joking reason I give for going out for the rest of the afternoon. But I am running away. I feel like running for my life.

Can Bel reasonably expect my love?

Ought I reasonably to love her? As in, for once be a kind, generous-spirited person first and foremost, rather than a career-focused writer?

It's just, depression is *so* unsexy.

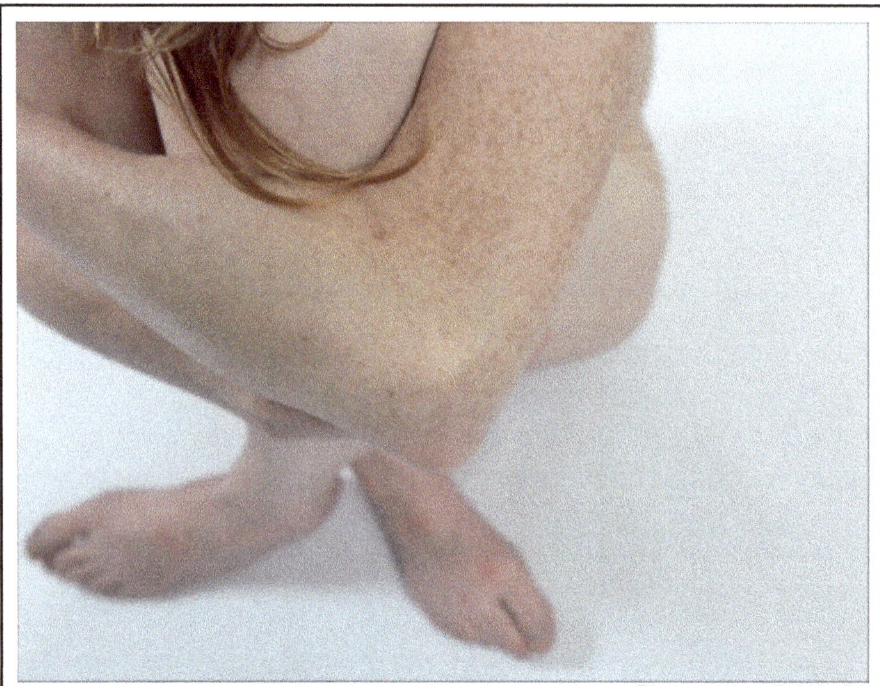

Photographer: **Fei Mo Di**

This picture is so beautiful. It dates back to my first week in Shanghai. How did I manage, all those months ago, to write off Fei Mo Di as a repulsive misogynistic public-school arsehole who hated me?

PART IV

The end

Unspoken goodbyes. At the street-side, beside the college's waiting airport car, Lily Hong flings herself against Bel like a puppy. 'Meet you at airport after fourteen days. Don't worry, be happy!'

'Be sure to get a chest x-ray,' I say, as I too give Bel a hug.

She gives a wooden one back. 'Fake.' Her grin is humourless. She gets into the car, and it drives away.

I feel sick. 'She's depressed enough to chuck herself out of the plane.'

'I don't understand,' says Lily Hong miserably. 'What mean depress, what mean chuck?'

'S'okay. Nothing.' I might never see Bel again. Paranoid thought? Anyway I don't know what to do or who to tell, so I go about my day as planned, heading out into the surreal half-light, what Bel calls the 'fake mist' – man-made, from filth - for my appointment.

Nanjing Road West. Starbucks. I come up behind Precocious Loiza, and see over her shoulder a familiar bondage photograph - a Japanese woman semi-clad in traditional robes, trussed up with rope and suspended.

'Oh!' She jumps, then - 'He-eyy!' - reaches to pull me down by the neck for a kiss on the lips.

'How's art college?' I hear a rasp in my own voice after sixty minutes of inhaling dirt.

Precocious Loiza points back at her iPad. 'This is the bag I've totally gotten into in my second semester at the Slade. I *love* Araki's work.'

I set down my rucksack, 'Can I get you another drink?'

'Tall skinny decaf latte thanks, and a biscotti. Wow, you've gone anorexic! Tamara says you were anorexic before she fed you up. In Year 10 at school we were forced to discuss this article about how very young models are coerced into retaining their pubescent shape instead of letting themselves physically

develop.[42] The school was, like, paranoid that we were all about
to starve ourselves. Mind you, two girls did die of eating
disorders but frankly they were loopy anyway and one of them
had been, like, raped. Amazing that you're starving yourself
even at your age - looks like you need Tamara again.'

'Yes. Gosh. No. I mean, great to see you. Back in a tick.'

Do I "need Tamara again"?

When I return with drinks, Precocious has unzipped a large
folio-carrier which she holds open to show me an enlargement
of one of her photos of me. 'For you. Tamara's got the same one
but three times bigger on the wall above her sofa.' Next, she
rummages in her leather tote bag. 'And she asked me to give
you this.'

It is a fat, weighty padded envelope, the top of which has
been firmly stapled closed. Bombarded, I feel limp; and
underlying that, a profound desolation. 'Thanks for all this
Loiza…'

'So what do you think of Araki? Do you know he has sex with
all his models? Like Picasso did, only with Araki it's a high
principle. He's, like, *totally* against objectification!' She reads off
from her iPad: '*Of course I had sex with all my models… I needed to
break down the me-and-you barrier. I can say that I have collapsed the
previous tradition of photography that emphasized objectivity. In the
past, photographers felt they had to eliminate their subjectivity as
much as possible. I consider myself a "subjective" photographer.*'[43]

Into my despondent silence the eighteen year-old suddenly orders –
'You should leave Shanghai. My parents have gone back to the UK.
They said they were being poisoned by the air and the food and that
nothing is safe.'

'People like me can't afford to live in the UK. I'm a loser in the UK.
Fucking neo-liberalism.'

'Embrace it! Marry someone rich - then England's awesome! I'm
going to.'

When I get home I open Tamara's envelope. It contains a
massive wad of 100 Yuan notes, and a note.

Photographer: **Precocious Loiza**[13]

This pic is Precocious Loiza's thank-you gift for my having been part of her Art A-level project. She got an 'A-star'. She hadn't shown me this one before. Kept it back as a surprise.

26th March
Saturday

Elise's funeral will take place tomorrow. My 'Hope you've arrived safely?' email to Bel has had no answer.

But I get distracted from my anxiety. Wonderfully. A one-off booking with an artist pal of Fei Mo Di devolves into a playful romp!

David Rodriguez' studio is in an attic in a dilapidated, picturesque 1930s low-rise apartment complex. It's only a few blocks as the crow flies from Aussie Cyril's villa, but this district has an altogether different character from the leafy elegance of Cyril's address. Lanes, alleyways, looping electrical cables; steep, dark wooden staircases; shared stone sinks on landings, washing lines and dangling wash-cloths, hubbub of family life in nooks and behind doors.

I reach the top of the house. His door is open, last night's lover just leaving – a pretty, childlike thing: long bony legs; wire-rimmed small, circular glasses on her cute nose; a whimsical straw bonnet.

David: Latin-American, laid-back, charming, disarming, his welcoming grin ear to ear.

I've met the other two models once before. Fei Mo Di made brief introductions at Trish Little's glitzy preview night a few weeks ago, then gossiped to me about them later. Alvira, a New Yorker, voluptuous, Afro-Caribbean heritage, Harvard-educated, feminist, lesbian, in Shanghai to start up a company manufacturing sex-toys. Wei Wei, Taiwanese, spent a dozen years in Paris, works in perfume design. Taiwan is very unlike China, pointed out Fei Mo Di, which is how come Wei Wei is able to be, in her behaviour, quite a Lee Miller type: uninhibited, free-thinking, liberated, and knowledgeable about the world, as well as elegant and beautiful.

Before the shoot starts we strip off and sit about, naked, comfortably warm – it is almost April - drinking Columbian espresso. I've got a lazy Saturday feeling that takes me back to my bedsit – hanging out with Tiffany. All my stresses temporarily lifted. The flat is three decrepit rooms filled with David's oil paintings hung randomly or leaning haphazardly on walls, none of which, he moans, have fully dried, due to the humidity. Is that why the medium of watercolour has always prevailed here?

Garulous Alvira puts David on the spot. 'So. Is this about race? About femaleness? Or are you into erotica? Do you want porn?'

'I do not know yet.' David puts his laptop on the table in front of us.

'I show you images of three women I found from other photographers. See this one - Terry Richardson is well known as erotic photographer so the idea to please men, the pleasure, is really a part of his choice. But this one here - a woman photographer - Ellen von Unwerth is more "two meanings".'

'Ambiguous,' offers Wei Wei.

'Yes yes yes. Every of you has English knowledge better than me. And next, John Currin: a part of his work is also relate to pornography… But it is also about *clichés*. See – it is complicated. I mean, is his motive ironic?'

We discuss all of this boisterously, drink coffee, crack sexist jokes, tease David. He breaks into our messing about, wanting to explain more.

'See here: these are artists' pictures of The Three Graces. In these classical paintings I cannot really say whether the idea was to please the looker, as we say now, but yes - most of these were painted by men.'

At last he picks up his camera. We are still sprawled, chatting, relaxing, pleasant window draught keeping at bay the first mosquitoes.

'So, my ladies, I do not think it is essential to remember those images, or those conventions, but I think we cannot ignore them neither. And as for the *voyeur* - the witness of these moments…

myself, the photographer... well, you must ignore me completely. I do not look for a special pose – no. What I want, very simple, it is to catch moments from the "interrelation" between three women. I am not asking you to please me somehow.'

Four nationalities. None of us mainland Chinese. A morning spent under a wooden roof with skylight views onto makeshift roof-gardens and rickety balconies and crammed-in house-fronts decorated with lines of washing strung like bunting. And yet we are disengaged from the world beyond David's rooms, from Shanghai and the Chinese, enjoying the solidarity of thrown-together aliens.

It does me good; for three hours, my worries suspended. We have such a laugh. I am ready to laugh, after yesterday's desolate goodbye.

Photographer: **David Rodriguez**

Columbian artist David Rodriguez employed me and two other women to do a shoot for 'The Three Graces', his project about the dynamic between threesomes of women.

How to go on surviving?

I have forward-planned for this afternoon. In my rucksack is the JG Ballard autobiography that Bel went on about, 'Miracles of Life': his 1930s childhood in Shanghai's elite international community followed by the gloom and doom of England. I will find a Starbucks and settle in.

Anything rather than return to the empty flat.

31ˢᵗ March
Thursday

No email from Bel. It is four days since the funeral. What has it done to her?

I'll email her one of these wacky pics from David's shoot. Maybe it'll stimulate a response.

Dear David,
Again – Gracias - a brilliant session! Fantastic pics – thanks for sending!
This one disturbs me though. Reminds me of Nazi concentration camps where people had to line up naked just like this to be photographed. Sorry for this macabre association. Call me paranoid. I think it's because yesterday afternoon I started reading JG Ballard's biography: he was in a brutal Japanese prison camp at Lunghua right here in Shanghai… Then later I was looking at my flatmate's books including war-photographer Lee Miller's photographs of the liberation of Buchenwald death camp. So I'm a bit too focused on human brutality at the moment.

Dear Suki,
SHANGHAI TURN ALL THE CREATIVE PEOPLE PARANOID OR CRAZY. Yes I know about the beautiful Lee Miller: I love the work of Man Ray! I try with his solarisation effect but not very successful. To get the effect by digital this is only fake. David x

Tuh - typical! Lee Miller recognised only as an appendage of Man Ray.

Dear David,
solarisation was Lee Miller's invention as much as Man Ray's. She does not get the recognition she deserves as a photographer. She photographed political assassinations. She photographed the suicided bodies of the mayor of Dresden and his wife and daughter. She's got loads more WW2 photos in a book I've got here

documenting bombed-out London.[44] *She took loads of photos of women at war*[45] *and women in the armed forces.*[46]
Suki

Dear Suki
I know that Lee Miller "not just a pretty face" (although, you know, she was *painted six times by Picasso). I know that she DID understood the Surrealist movement – she must, she married a Surrealist painter Roland Penrose. His work I think kitsch and "derivative" so I am not surprise he became only an organiser/administrator at end. By the way, I have email conversation with the man now Director of Exhibitions at Penrose's "glorious foundation", your Institute of Contemporary Arts in London. I pitch an exhibition concept to him. Say to me good luck!*

Dear David,
Picasso didn't paint pretty faces.
Best of British luck with your ICA pitch!
Actually I've always thought it a bit weird that Roland Penrose got off with Lee Miller. As a pacifist and conscientious objector, how could he be together with someone whose adrenalin was fired (maybe even enthusiasm is the word) by seeking out and capturing human brutality on film?

I love sparring with fellow-creatives - something that doesn't work with Aussie Cyril, my wet, malleable, acquiescent devotee.

Afternoon. Another session with Cyril.

I sip at his ginger latte, force myself to consider the positives. Melbourne has no brutal war history, no concentration camps. The sun is always shining. I could live off Cyril and write without having to find paid work. No more modelling!

After each pose he pops a truffle into my mouth.

Could I be plump and happy with this doting man?

Before bed, a final check for emails, texts. Nothing from Bel, despite the pic I sent.

Wonder if she's had her chest x-ray?
Maybe that's it. This silence. She's found out she's got cancer.

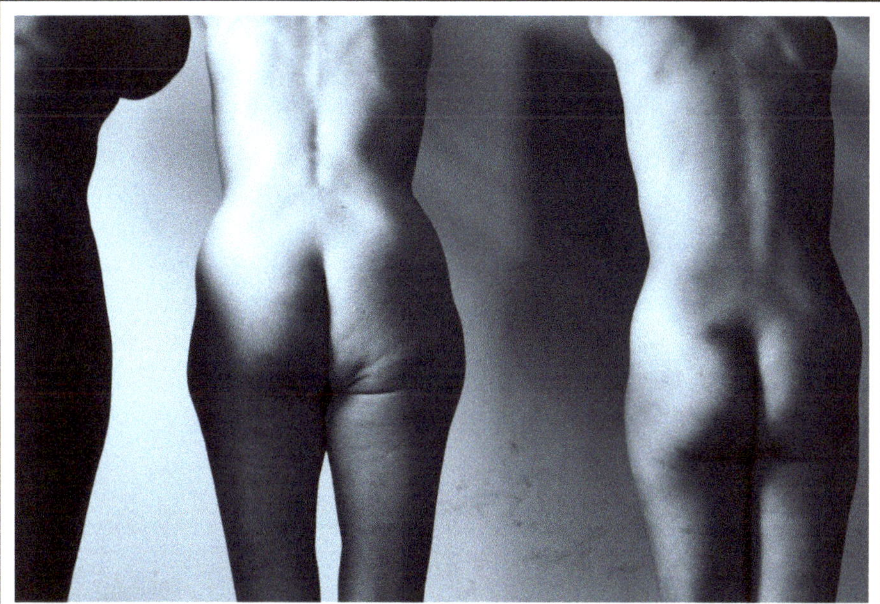

Photographer: **David Rodriguez**

Have I 'gone anorexic', as Loiza commented? My backside in this photo by David Rodriguez looks hideously puckered. What can I do, though? I can't jog in this pollution. Must eat even less.

April Fool's Day
Friday 1ˢᵗ April

My dearest Much-More-Than-Muse Suki -
Yesterday's shoot was wonderful. Boy, that was a long time of
concentration... Wiped me out. A very intense five hours! We
worked hard, thought hard, shared lots of ideas, achieved great
things. I loved it. Lots of interesting poses, angles, etc... Perhaps
you'll find me a sentimental old fool for sending this one along first,
but there is something very special about this photo; the completely
relaxed directness... For me, it is close to some of Rembrandt's,
suggesting a mysterious moment; a strange sectioning of time.
Strange also because I arrived at this via an intriguing colour
version and then a very different black and white, and then
experimenting with more contrast...
It will grow on you.
Cyril

I hate the pic he has attached.

But it's great I managed to spin out the session for five hours.
He pays me an hourly rate.

I have no money left apart from what is in Tamara's envelope.

Dear Cyril,
The breast has to go. There is simply no reason to have a naked
breast on a study of an ugly-but-interesting face. The naked breast
makes this picture tacky, tawdry and embarrassing. My version
makes my right eye the focus, by cropping to just above my collar-
bone. See attached. As you know, I rarely like photos of my face,
whereas an artwork depicting me is a different matter: I have more
distance to those; I don't care so much about how "I" look, because
drawings or paintings say probably more about the artist than they
do about me.
S

Suki.

Is your cropped version an April Fool's joke? It is a crying shame to crop it as you have done. I cannot see anything tacky or tawdry. My intention is to depict the model's personality. This seems to me an incredibly tender but very honest portrait. I think it beautiful. If I were a real artist I might hang a 5-foot version of it in my living room.
Your
Cyril

Cyril –
As said, there is no reason for this picture to be a nude in order to communicate the model's personality. In my opinion the picture is about the face - and also, compositionally, the lovely arm and hand positions. It is simply tawdry for this older, serious-looking woman to be naked. In this picture I am neither (a) beautiful, nor (b) interesting for being hideously grotesque. The breast is extraneous, hence embarrassing. My crop turns it into a straightforward portrait. I don't want to be 100% negative. I appreciate that you paid so much attention to getting this image to black and white, which is self-evidently far more effective than the colour version.
Suki

I am tired of this non-stop email courtship by Cyril.

Why nothing from Bel? Could my theory be right? A chest x-ray that showed up something terrible?

She's been gone seven days. Without Bel, what is my *raison d'etre*, here in Shanghai?

I am an April fool.

Bel, pls let me know how things are going. Hard time for you. Take care Sxx

Photographer: Aussie Cyril

A portrait by Cyril. *Bleagh,* disgusting. I've had to crop it.

3rd April
Sunday

One more week til Bel's return. I am pleased with myself that I am managing alone. I have lost 2.3 kilos. I email Mike Little and Fei Mo Di to organize the launch of 'Qi Qi's life-room'[47] before Bel's return so she doesn't have to suffer a social occasion. Yes - me, mustering a party! Does this mean I *do* have friends in Shanghai?

At last I tidy up. Strewn all around the flat are print-outs of articles that Bel has found important. The fuel for her apocalyptic visions. I pile the sheets on her desk. Or should I bin them?

I skim through the familiar 'anti-neoliberalism' one by Pankaj Mishra.[40]

> '...*More and more people feel the gap between the profligate promises of individual freedom and sovereignty, and the incapacity of their political and economic organisations to realise them... Frustration tends to be highest in countries that have a large population of educated young men ... find themselves unable to fulfil the promise of self-empowerment... For many of them, the contradiction has become intolerable.*'

The next paragraph has *China!!!* written in the margin:

> '...*Xi Jinping and other demagogues of developing countries deploy... jingoistic nationalism and cross-border militarism as a valve for domestic tensions...*'

There's more about the Chinese government's "self-legitimizing narrative": a hybrid of national heritage, i.e. Mao-plus-Confucius...

'…They have also retro-fitted old-style nationalism for their growing populations of uprooted citizens, who harbour yearnings for belonging and community as well as material plenitude.'

This is happening right here, where I am. I look out over the university campus's high wall, see the bolted-together uniform metal huts along along its perimeter. You see them everywhere. Housing for the new migrants. Dormitories with shared outdoor hot water taps and a toilet block. Country folk who are marshalled into building the new apartment blocks, but can then only hopelessly stare up at them. The 'good life' fairytale is far out of reach for so many people.

I can't read more of this worrisome stuff. I retreat to the bedroom, my makeshift desk, my iPad.

God. Another email from Cyril. Don't know if I can bear him any more.

Darling Suki,
a propos *your remarks about portraits of you by artists being easier to distance yourself from than photographs: I have been browsing online and found various painted portraits of you by several of your former employers which unkindly make you look masculine. I do not understand how you can be unperturbed by such as these, while rejecting my photographs in which you look so beautiful.*

Sigh. He doesn't get it. He doesn't get me.

Cyril, I like looking like a man.

I don't send it.
Ping! An email arriving from Bel!

It's sent from her phone. No words, just a link – uncanny, I can hardly believe it - to this same Pankaj Mishra article. Telepathy? At least she's alive - but still obsessing over bad news.

Hi Bel, how did the funeral go? Are you okay? How are you?

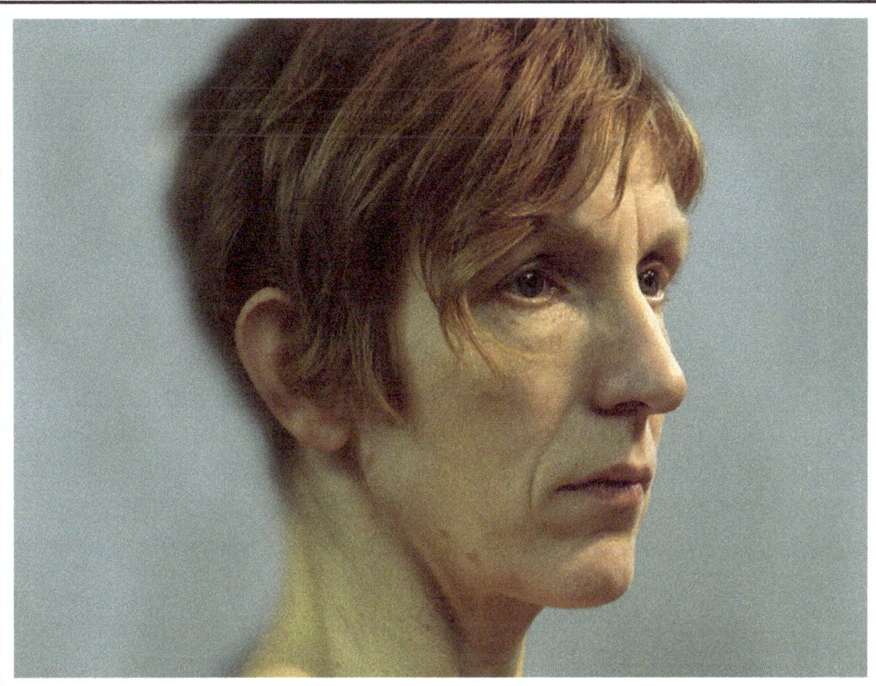

Photographer: **Tom Wood**

The point of including this photo is to educate Aussie Cyril. Artist Tom Wood, who took the photo, has painted me looking like a boy lots of times.

5th April
Tuesday evening

Dear Artists and friends of Bel! Party at Qi Qi's Café Bar, tomoz 8pm, to launch Bel's fantastic 'Qi Qi's Life-room' movie[47] - some of you are its stars! Be there or be square! All welcome, pls spread word. Suki x

It's a full turn-out.

Mike Little has chipped in with champagne and canapés, and has got some press representatives to come along. Trish has over-excitedly parcelled her bulky form into a black satin evening gown topped off with a net-festooned purple hat. Besides Greg-I'm-a-Kiwi and his artist friends there are half a dozen Art Nude group members, including Cyril, who inevitably heard on the grapevine, plus a bunch of Fei Mo Di's designer friends and Alvira, Wei Wei, Qi Qi, Lily Hong…

Where's Bel? Everyone asks. It feels strangely like a Bel memorial event.

Lily Hong pats my arm, as though comforting me: 'She come back soon. Three days.'

As if I'm not counting.

How ironic, that a circle of international arty friends seems to have crystallized since Bel left.

Could I stay on here, after all?

Midnight. A drunken conversation between die-hards Cyril and Greg-I'm-a-Kiwi who are propping up the bar. Photographers, sex, relationships, sex.

'…Whereas Lee Miller, being both model and photographer, is totally outside the box.' Greg drains another pint of Vedett Extra Blond. 'She's hard to categorize. Like, I totally agree with the photographer Duane Michals, that the nude figure implies both vulnerability and sex; but Miller, as a woman - whether as nude model, or as photographer of the nude - well…' he sets down his glass – 'she may not have seen either vulnerability or sex as part of the equation.'

'Vulnerability and sex?' I knock back the rest of my glass. 'She'd certainly have disagreed with you about sex being automatically implied by nudity. Nakedness can be *so* unsexy. As for vulnerability – in my experience there's a paradoxical combination in nudity of both vulnerability and strength.'

Cyril is hunched over a Jack Daniels. 'I share Michals' view that the photographer of the nude is intensely aware of the presence of the body and is taking pleasure in looking at the body.'

'Ha – honesty at last!' I stab a finger at Cyril. 'You're motivated by sex, not Art.'

'I'm simply quoting Michals' words.' Drunk, Cyril reveals a totally different side of himself. Assertive. 'The viewer of the nude inevitably "responds out of a sexual curiosity".'[21]

'Rubbish. That would mean, no gay guy would be motivated to photograph a female nude. So Robert Mapplethorpe disproves that, for a start.'

'That perv,' Cyril snorts nastily.

'I think Michals was gay,' Greg chips in. 'He produced at least one gay-themed picture-series.'

I guzzle at my wine (Changyu dry red, fourth glass). 'To get back to Lee Miller – did you know she was into polyamory before the term had even been coined? As in, she actively encouraged her lovers to have other lovers.'

'Loada crap,' Cyril growls from his corner.

'And obviously she didn't expect her lovers to have a problem with her sleeping with others.'

'My second wife was full of that shit.'

'Well, I personally would like the kind of marriage Lee had with Roland Penrose. They let each other sleep with whoever they wanted.'

Cyril knocks back his whisky. 'As a matter of fact, the agreement between Lee and Penrose was that their love for each other would remain "sacred" – as in, they would be absolutely faithful in that respect. They just permitted each other to sleep around. Which is still a loada crap.' Cyril looks directly at me. 'I mean, what does wife mean, if not "belongs to husband"?'

I look directly back at him: elderly, fat, slumped; his chin almost resting on the bar.

6th April
Wednesday, 8 a.m.

Dring dring!
The sun too bright. Jeezus. I crawl from bed to answer the landline. It's Lily Hong.
'Oh. Lily. Think my head's going to explode. How's yours?'
'Miss Suki, please come now. We wait you in Foreign Affairs Office.'
Lily Hong stands up when I walk in, her lip trembling at me like a little girl's. The Director of Foreign Affairs gently tells me they have received news that my colleague Bel is 'deceased'.

I am then left for some time.

By myself.

Peace and quiet.

The office is very simple.

After a while, green tea is served.

It is late evening when I finally get a message to your brother. I have to go on your laptop – sorry - and look in your contacts for his email address.
John.

It takes him more than 24 hours to reply.

Greg-I'm-a-Kiwi experiments with interesting settings or situations for nudes; stuff that suggests a back-story. He says this photo is *après* Duane Michals, most of whose work isn't Art Nude; Michals worked as a fashion photographer on Vogue etc. A lot of Michals' photographs have a hinted-at if not strong narrative, which is what Greg has aimed for in this photo.

9ᵗʰ April
Saturday

Just checking your emails again. S'okay, none are personal. Just spam and stuff.

'Scuse me while I check my own emails. Oh! - your brother again:

> *...basic details are, one week after her daughter's funeral Bella took Élise's ashes onto the Ostend-to-Dover ferry to scatter them at sea. Remarkably Élise had managed to write a note asking for this, indicating a rare moment of rationality. The note compounded the tragedy for Bella by proving Élise's suicide was pre-meditated.*
> *... passengers saw Bella jump, but the rescue was not quick enough to save her life...*
> *...have no idea about a chest x-ray. Are you sure? She never mentioned...*

I think John thinks I'm just the person you were sharing a flat with.

I suppose he's not wrong.

And here's a long email from my ex, Ilka!... Well well... She's going to marry a 72 year-old widower who likes art, because she's lonely. I'll just quickly acknowledge it:

> *Dear Ilka – CONGRATS! Wishing you peace & contentment & hope ul be happy. He sounds good person. No need get defensive about going straight. Have had marriage offer myself. New life in Australia. But need my independence. To be honest sth horrible hs happened here will write more v soon not now. Sx*

We're wondering, Bel - did you leave us a note? I've been searching this desk, but there's nothing much... My last poetry collection;[48] a couple more books: 'Chinese Whispers' by Ben Chu, 'The Good Earth' by Pearl Buck; all these print-outs of articles that I've kept for you in a neat stack... You've put a big red circle round a paragraph on this first one, the Paul Verhaeghe:

> *'…the freedom we perceive ourselves as having in the west is the greatest untruth of this day and age… We are forever told that we are more free to choose the course of our lives than ever before, but the freedom to choose outside the success narrative is limited. Furthermore, those who fail are deemed to be losers or scroungers, taking advantage of our social security system.'*

Exactly what Tim Lott[29] said. The culture of our homeland sets us up for terminal frustration, disappointment and a sense of failure.

I, too, hate this world. But as you say - which corner of the planet to run to?

Photographer: **Bel**

When I went onto your laptop on Wednesday night I discovered you'd installed this pic as the screensaver. One from your movie about me, 'Still Life',[49] made soon after we first met. I look then how I now feel. Was I having a premonition about you? Is there such a thing as a 'suicidal nature', and did I sense it?

13th April
Wednesday

I've lost you. I've lost Ilka for good, too. And I've lost sight of my manuscript.

What has Shanghai done for me?

What did it do for you?

Dear Suki,
Thank you for all your assistance in my communications with Bella's Shanghai employers in the last week. Thank you also for boxing up and posting Bella's possessions, I am most grateful. I will of course refund all postage via your UK account if you could please provide your bank details – thanks. Pls let me know how many boxes will eventually be in the post and the approximate date of arrival. Below is a link to Bella's obituary from the Guardian in case you have not seen it. The Guardian is one of the newspapers which used to publish Bella's photographs.
Thanks again for your assistance at this sad time.
Best wishes, John

Did you find out you were terminally ill, Bel, so decided to kill yourself? Was it not really about your daughter, or anything else? Did you not, after all, have it all planned before you left me? Or was a cancer diagnosis just a laughable irony considering your intention to leave this sick planet anyway?

Your obituary is an eye-opener. Born in Surrey. Dutch father, Polish mother. Guildford Grammar School. Kibbutz before Cambridge. Dropped out of English Literature to go travelling with artist husband Eli Esteban in the Middle East, *...an odyssey that stimulated Bella's award-winning career in war journalism which brought an early end to the marriage. Their only child, Elise, was brought up by paternal family members. Bella's recent loss of her daughter...*

With this information I've been doing searches on you all night. Scouring for more details. Finding images. You, in dusty camouflage gear. Harrowing photos from Afghanistan.

What did I know about you before? Unsettled. Questing. Idealistic. Brave. A love-child made with a stranger. Private.

Why did you keep so much to yourself? Jewish. Divorced. Award-winning. Your daughter died by hanging herself. A medal for bravery.

Was your accidental child the reason why your marriage ended? And did you tell your in-laws of their grandchild's true parentage? Maybe they knew, but were compassionate. A child's a child.

Veiled, hidden person - it's not my fault I failed to love you. "Whatever that means".

Another Guardian Online obit, referenced in the sidebar, catches my attention: *Astronaut Ludowic Kendal dies aged 87, Cornwall…*

But I must crack on with sorting out your stuff. Your PC is just waking up from sleep mode. There: your qq account's now on-screen. Dozens of un-opened emails. What am I supposed to do about them? I don't know how to close down a life. I have no experience.

Desk clearance is more straightforward. I'm binning all your printed-out articles, packing the handful of books into one of the half-filled boxes. I see my poetry collection has a page-corner turned down.

Christ, Bel. That poem's about suicide.[50] *Were* you thinking of it?

The college's *Waiban* has issued me a deadline of fourteen days to leave the flat. I hate being here anyway. Empty of you. Empty of your stuff. Empty of food. The stench in the kitchen increasingly retch-inducing.

I want to hear you ranting about another imminent catastrophe. I'll pay better attention. Promise. Please come back.

Afternoon. Your students have been enjoying the cancellations of their classes.

Poor, miserable Lily Hong has just helped me book my flight. We're on our way now to visit an exhibition - Cyril's recommendation - by the photographer Ai Do. But on the Metro she's inconsolable. What can I do?

'Bel my best friend [sob]. I speak Bel all my sorrow [sob]. I lonely now.'

I can't help her, Bel. Your lover. In mourning.

She is suddenly direct. 'Bel speak me *her* sorrow too.' Her stern eyes, her tone… I'm being told off. '"Suki is closed", Bel say me. "Suki is self-obsess". Means Bel can't speak you her sorrow. So she speak me her sorrow.'

For the rest of the way I am speechless. Should I chuck myself off this fly-over?

Until in the gallery Lily Hong breaks down again. 'My father at prison.'

'Oh god – I didn't know. That's awful.'

'Not bad man! Government say he corruption. Every businessman corruption. He only same. Government make example.'

'Is there anything I can do?' Stupidest question in the world.

She trails after me into the gallery café, slumps mournfully at a table. What to do, Bel? I am rubbish at this. Like I was rubbish at taking care of you. I get her a latte.

She looks up at me. 'I want to go outside China, start new life.'

'Where do you want to go? How?'

'I tell Bel I want marry a foreigner, but she say "all men are bastards". Not help me.'

'Hmm…'

Look, Bel. Sometimes pragmatism can work for people. This is what I can offer her.

'…would an Australian be okay?'

On the Metro home I notice a new text. It's always ridiculously disappointing when I see it's not from you.

Dear Suki – saw Guardian obit for your Bel – my god, what's going on? You must be in shock! Can I do anything?
Tamara

God. Tamara. I haven't even acknowledged her own bereavement.

Photographer: **Aussie Cyril**

Cyril took this on his phone and gave it a 'magic lantern' effect.

23rd April
Saturday

It's three weeks since you died. I am in the French Concession without you and am lost. In the sense of, unanchored. I could end up anywhere.

I forgot to charge my phone overnight so I find it dead in the bottom of my bag, but even if it were not dead, I cannot check in with you like I normally would do; let you know my whereabouts. My touchstone, my protector, here in Shanghai.

So here I am in a poky vintage tea-room, Edwardian-style: mirrors, chandeliers, oak panelling, deep plummy draperies and half-darkness. Once I'd stepped in to find out where the quaint entrance led to, I got ushered – so was too embarrassed to leave. So here I am, drinking lemon tea in place of lunch. A strange, absolute solitude in seething Shanghai. 'Solitude is only physical whereas loneliness is a mental pain.' I wrote that when I was fifteen.

Back in the flat I pick up Cyril's latest email offering. Once sober, he is his usual docile, pedagogic, avuncular self.

Darling Suki, I do hope you love this snap of you as much as I do. It is après *Jeanloup Sieff. Sieff and others started to look for and celebrate the model's personality, giving a final 'up yours' to the academic art world wherein the nude had always been elevated to the realm of the exotic, classical or sentimental; a realm in which the nude must never come across as "herself" - a real, individual personality. Your thoughts?*

And can we please meet to talk about our future, since you imminently have to change abodes? Much, much love, Cyril xxx

Dear Cyril,
why did you take the colour out? Bel was really against turning photos into black and white. She said it was fake nostalgia. Have you seen the most expensive photograph ever to be sold?[51] A dramatic landscape, reproduced in black and white, bought in 2010.

As Bel said, in the end it's just an arty special effect in Photoshop. Anyone can do it. Suki

His response, as always, is immediate. He spends his life waiting on me.

My dearest Suki. You had something special with Bel, didn't you. You never explained… I am sorry for my lack of understanding. I am truly sorry for your loss.
If there is anything I can do… Well, you know.
All my love,
Cyril
Please let us meet

Ping! A reply from Ilka!

Dear Suki – "need my independence"? Don't you really mean, "incapable of committing"? Your problem is, you are incapable of submitting and letting the journey of a fellow-traveller alter the path of your own life. Oblivious to the needs of anyone you are with, you gallop on relentlessly (randomly, chaotically) on your so-called "quest". You are all about your own survival. You are not able to support anyone else, because you just move on and on.
   Accept the marriage proposal! That's my advice. Ilka

She's right, isn't she, Bel.

Dear Ilka, I cant look afta anyone. Emotionally. Or cooking. Hav failed badly. Deep regret. Suki

Photographer: **Aussie Cyril**

Cyril says this informal snap after one of our sessions is akin to fashion photographer Jeanloup Sieff's personality-portraying nudes, contrasting to the sterile poses in which fashion models are typically placed. Like Duane Michals, Sieff also worked in fashion photography, which was very much about stylized, uniform 'ideal types'. His nudes, however, are exceptional because his photographs retain the models' particular identities even when their faces are not shown - achieving 'a perceptive feeling of intimacy' (to quote, as always, the dog-eared Peter Lacey paperback borrowed from Cyril).[34] Cyril informed me that our "Great British Institution" Sir Kenneth Clark once made the bald claim that the erotic is, and must always be, present in the nude. In the nineteen-sixties, two topics of heated debate were: whether or not the erotic is pornographic, and also, more significantly, the contention of the establishment that photography did not and could not quite attain the level of fine art. Whatever; these guys Michals and especially Sieff were at last showing the nude model "as she is".

I must admit I like this one by Cyril. At least he's distracting me from things.

24th April
Sunday

Dear Fei Mo Di, I want to achieve one last thing in Shanghai. For Bel. She wanted Still Life, the first movie she completed here, to have Chinese subtitles.[49] Have you got time?'

Hi Suki – okay I can do it. Miraculously I'm free today. One condition: we do one final shoot together. Outdoors. This morning. Now. Ok? FMD

So he has shown up at the campus: very spontaneous, very Shanghainese, a fresh daisy in the vase of his Volkswagen Beetle, and is driving us to a woodland outside the city. We bicker for the entire journey - companionable, mates-together bickering (- in truth, we have so much in common), and the scenery and freshness is lovely. Now I am naked in the wilderness, climbing trees, lying in bracken. Fei Mo Di despises breasts and excess flesh and loves my newly skeletal form. He produces a picnic lunch from a wicker hamper: strawberries; elderflower cordial. We are in a Merchant Ivory movie. It is heaven.

Late afternoon.
Back at Fei Mo Di's pristine penthouse we work like Trojans, zinging on espressos, until your subtitles are completed and superimposed onto the movie and the whole thing uploaded for the world to view.
Our flat, when he drops me back here, is ugly: the massive, never-used Chinese TV; grubby whitewashed walls spattered with small red messes of swatted mosquitoes. Our things are all gone: everything boxed up ready to post tomorrow, or already piled beside my suitcase in readiness for my day-after-tomorrow flight. I sit on the hard wooden bench devoid of your cushions and automatically waken your iPad to check the world's news – but then I can't face it.

I am seated, reading, my loneliness almost delicious, when a Skype call sings out of the iPad.

'Tamara! Hey - great!' The signal is strong for once. She looks terrific.

'You're crying.'

'No. Yes. Coz I'm reading about Lee Miller's life again. Comparing her to Bel.'

'*And* you're frighteningly scrawny. This is worrying. I'm going to put you on a diet.'

'This book[15] - it describes Lee at the end of her life as "a soul in hell, cut off from the work and the life she loved" due to alcoholism, drug abuse, manic depression and creative frustration.'

'That doesn't sound like Bel's state.'

'She was really obsessed with Lee, though. I'm just looking for… trying to understand. Lee's son says she lost her looks after his birth and that's when she really degenerated into a slob, and got really difficult and quarrelsome. In the end she was a total mess: alcoholic, obsessive, frumpy, entirely in the shadow of her husband who'd made himself a VIP in the art world – you know, the guy who started the ICA?'

'Your Bel was an independent woman. Still working and functioning. But clearly she had some long-term mental health issues.'

'She'd become really depressed… anxious… introverted…'

'Suki. You've just spent half a year holding the hand of a dying person.'

'I was useless at getting her to talk…'

'You are remarkable.'

[sob] 'I just don't understand it…'

'You need some looking-after now. Which it is my privilege to offer. It's ten months since you left Engl…'

Crash. 'Aagh!'

'Suki! What the..?'

I'm on my feet - 'Christ!'

Tamara's voice - 'You've gone dark - '

I reach for the wall to steady myself.

'Are you alright?'

'The electricity's out - the iPad's on batteries. I think the meter box just exploded –

'I saw a flash – ?'

'The metal front panel's gone flying across the room; there's wiring and stuff from inside it scattered about in bits …'

'But you're okay? Are you okay?'

'I'm intact, thanks; honest.'

'Is anything on fire?'

'Don't worry! Look, I need to call someone - I've got no electricity. I need to call a staff member. Got to go.'

I am waiting in the dark for Lily Hong. Jeezus Christ, if I'd been sitting over there instead of here…

A *Eureka!* moment: I've just learned I don't want to die.

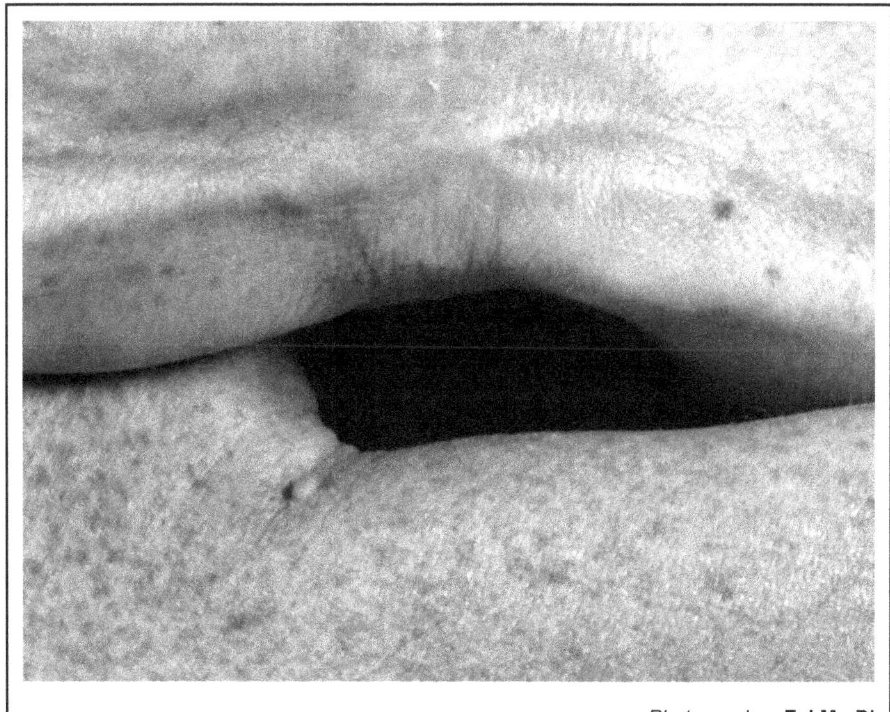

Photographer: **Fei Mo Di**

25th April
Monday morning

I'm going to marry you. This will stop you from taking off again and make you write. In two days you will be at a desk in my apartment with your exciting new manuscript. Can't tell you how much am looking forward. Tamara

'I'm getting married!'

The apartment block's landing is bright and sunny. I am perched on a stool outside my flat in order to use an electrical socket to power my netbook, and to receive internet access from a teacher across the hall who has kindly given me her password.

The *Waiban* has not repaired the flat's electricity since the fuse-box exploded. They are keen to see the back of me. I am not, after all, an employee. Without you here, Bel, I am nobody. No electricity means I have no hot water for a shower, no landline, no cooker or microwave or means of making a cup of tea. The fridge-freezer is dead and defrosting onto the floor-tiles. But I don't care; I've given up on food, anyway, and tomorrow is my flight.

At Tamara's I will write, write, write. The novel, then Part III of my trilogy, then the next thing, and the next. The trick is, Bel, to not let the world's looming crises encroach on your inner life. I will blot it all out. Maybe Tamara will take me to live in the country…

Afternoon.

Lily Hong shows up to help me carry seven cardboard boxes from the flat into a waiting taxi. She looks me up and down appraisingly. 'Legs like bird legs. Break if you not careful. You need eat lot of rice.' She leans across the small lake in which the fridge-freezer is now swimming, plucks from its door a tattered paper taped onto it, and stumblingly reads aloud my poem.

'The survivors.

> Stick-thin hipless bare-balconied oblong,
> up top a penthouse's smoked-glass pyramid,
> at the foot topiary peacocks, a marble portico.
> Its many square eyes stare down,
> dark spectacles framed in chrome,
> to where frogs chirrup and giggle
> in a landscaped swamp among peonies,
> willow, a large palm, privet cut in shapes.
>
> On the day these blank-looking smoothed-off faces
> rupture with black yowls, the day this concrete
> topples into the car-parks, when girders snap
> like breadsticks and cars get hammered flat,
> when doors unhinge while lethal dust plumes up,
>
> on that day these frogs will belly-flop happily
> into the water pooling afresh among severed cables,
> utility pipes up-ended, broken glass, detritus.
> Across the trashed city these wide-lipped fat frogs
> will plop goggle-eyed into water-holes, barking happily,
> not squashed dead under rubble but smiling
> slit-mouthed, fleshy-bottomed, belching happily
> then belly-laughing in this freshly re-created world
> amid the lushly-rotting corpses, succulents,
> humidity, the vivid greenery.'[52]

She finally looks across at me. 'Not understand all words. Some words.'

'You did great! Thank you. You did great. Really. Your English has really improved.'

She doesn't beam, these days; just looks care-worn. How old is she, in fact? Perhaps, setting aside the frills and bows, mid-thirties?

'Please could you come to the post office with me, Lily Hong? I must be sure that these two boxes go to England – *Yinguo* - and the other five go to Antwerp, and I need a receipt.'

'Of course I come with you!' - at last she beams. 'You help me a lot: promise find me husband!'

A final issue to deal with.

> *Dear Cyril,*
> *pls – a favour. Cd you meet up with Bel's former colleague Lily Hong – that pretty girl you noticed at Trish Little's preview? See her contact details below. She's on Wechat. She wants to marry a foreigner and start a new life outside China. I think she likes photography. Well, selfies. Hope you hit it off. I wish you a happy return to Australia.*
> *Suki x*
> *PS I can't marry you myself. Sorry. Am marrying someone else.*

Photographer: **Bel**

This is my favourite by Bel. I look like Alice in Wonderland. She took it while making the movie 'Under the Gaze'.[36]

50
27th April
Wednesday

It is seven and a half months since I arrived here, at this airport perpetually seething with people. I'm squatted on the floor, reaching the end of Bel's Christmas book.[16] God - I'd find it impossible, having one Chinese and one British parent like Ben Chu does. How the hell do you behave, when you come from two – well, almost like, two species?

The final page. I'm skimming it while shuffling slowly forwards in the queue for boarding. My head is itchy (unwashed hair). My clothes are manky too. I probably stink a bit.

The man in front - British, suit-and-tie, middle-aged, big-bellied, wheezing – scowls in an obvious way at my book's title 'Chinese Whispers: why everything you've heard about China is wrong', then turns away, handing his young Chinese wife his emptied MacDonalds paper-cup-with-straw for her to dispose of.

Despair of humanity comes over me too easily.

Meanwhile Ben Chu is telling off his readers. 'Start thinking of the Chinese not as some homogenous and intimidating mass of humanity, but as individuals...' The peasanty-looking Chinese guy behind me starts pushing – like, we're all going to get on the plane faster if you do that.

'...There are good and bad people among them, just as anywhere else', writes Chu.

'Some are corrupt, some upright. Some are brutal, some compassionate. Some are greedy, some frugal. Some are mean, some generous. Some are racist, some are tolerant. Some are narrowly nationalist, some are voraciously cosmopolitan.'

It's high time, says Ben Chu, that we all moved beyond Somerset Maugham's inability to empathise.

I admit, I'm crap at empathy. Too quick to write people off as hopelessly alien when they don't behave like me. Useless at fathoming another person's mind.

Once buckled into my seat by the window, I return to the final page that I've only skimmed, because I am keen to learn.

'There is no unfathomable Chinese mind ... There really is no Chinese mystery waiting to be revealed...'

I have to pause from reading to do my usual thing of manically gripping the arm-rests for the few moments of take-off – those seconds when the wheels leave the ground and you get tilted back as the plane soars steeply upwards...

The wheels tuck in and clunk somewhere. I dare to peer down at the receding city lights, feeling the plane judder as though bumping into the curb, but no – there is no curb; it's just air. Then back to the book in my lap. The final sentence.

'To understand the Chinese, we need only listen to our own hearts.'

A flare in the corner of my eye. Below the plane a beautiful orange peony is blooming. No – a tangerine cloud, billowing towards us; no - a red flag unfurling until it entirely covers the sky and now turns spangled - the eruption of a white-hot firework display.

Exclamations fill the quiet of the plane - on my side only, the side from which the windows of the sideways-tilted and slowly-arcing jumbo jet have been offering a glittering cityscape until this fireball. Now hubbub; now urgent calling across the rows to other belted-in passengers who cannot see outside, until the fantastically-evolving light-show has a soundtrack – a clamour of excited exchanges, calls to the stewards, wails. Seconds become a half-minute, the multilingual cacophony of agitation building, unintelligible, now harmonizing into a collective keen. The jet distances itself from the city, then from the haze of electric lights defining the outer metropolis. Above the racket, an urgent-sounding announcement in Chinese begins. Distant human settlements are coming into view, speckling the darkness like far-away galaxies, while the receding tremendous ball of flame above central Shanghai has gained dark edges of nothingness; no lights from the city's heart, all the glitter gone.

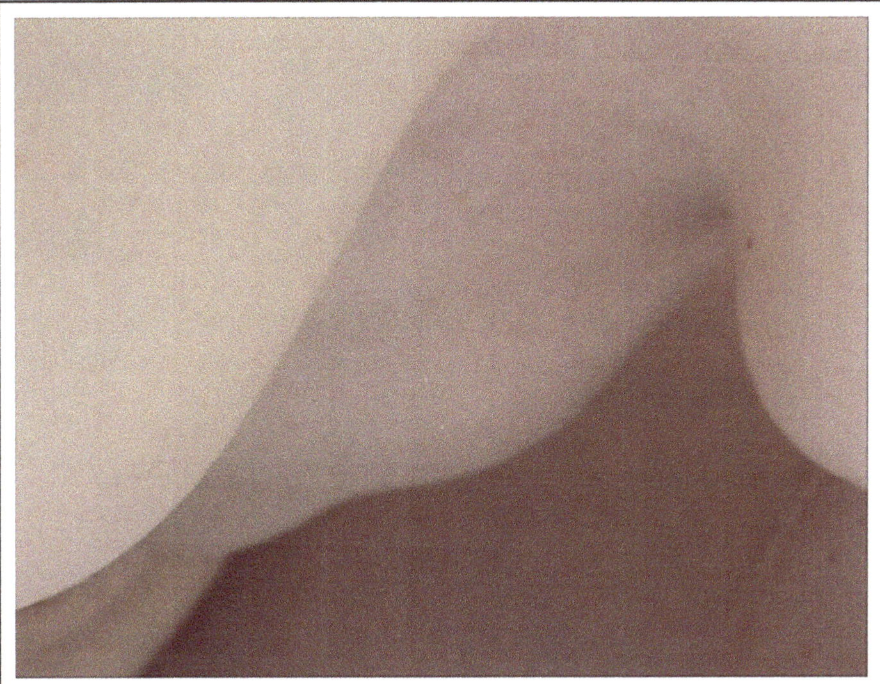

Photographer: **Fei Mo Di**

Fei Mo Di was slaving the last two days, he said, to finish this amazing movie for me, 'S', as a goodbye gift. This photo is taken from it. We promised each other we'd meet up in London for cake at Maison Berteaux on Greek Street. Soon.

Notes

1. Anton Büller is a fictitious character. The original painting (of which this is a detail) is by Yorkshire-based UK artist Tony Bulley. See *flickr.com/photos/tonybulley*

2. Google Adrian Searle's criticism of the art of Euan Uglow: *Must try softer*, in 'The Guardian' newspaper (8 July 2003)

3. Photographer Mike Kilyon has provided the images used for the fictitious characters of Hong Kong Ron, Bel, and Mike Little. See *mikekilyon.co.uk*

4. Karen L Kleinfelder's thesis has been published as an illustrated book: ,The Artist, His Model, Her Image, His Gaze' (University of Chicago Press 1993)

5. Google Sean O'Hagan's article *Photography is Art and always will be*, in 'The Guardian' newspaper (11 December 2014)

6. Quotation from an online excerpt taken from Susan Sontag's book 'On Photography' (Penguin, London, 1979). To read the excerpt, go to susansontag.com (excerpt dated 1977).

7. Lise Vogel's essay *Fine Arts and feminism: The Awakening Consciousness*, appears in 'Feminist Art Criticism: an anthology', Raven, Langer, Frueh (eds.), UMI Research Press, Ann Arbor, 1988

8. Check out Fergus Ryan: **Chinese mock claims Beijing is most liveable city despite smog lifting, in 'The Guardian' newspaper (22 Aug 2015)**

9. Quotation from Becky E. Conekin's book, 'Lee Miller in Fashion' (Thames and Hudson, London, 2013)

10. UK-based South African photographer Lloyd Spencer has provided the images used for the fictitious character of Aussie Cyril. See *flickr.com/people/lloydspencer*, also *theheartofleeds.com*

11. UK musician and artist Phil Moody has provided the images used for the fictitious character of Fei Mo Di. See *philmoody.com*

12. Yorkshire-based UK photographer Rod Jackson has provided the images used for the fictitious character of Jacques-from-Brussels.

13. UK-based Canadian-born artist Lois Brothwell has provided the images used for the fictitious character of Loiza. See *loizart.co.uk*

14. 'Two Small Lives' by Suki (Naked Eye Publishing, England, 2016) is Part II of her autobiography, the prequel to this current volume. It may be read in full online at *twosmalllives.co.uk*.

15. Prose, Francine: 'The lives of the muses: nine women and the artists they inspired' (Union Books, 2013)

16. Chu, Ben: 'Chinese whispers – why everything you've heard about China is wrong' (Weidenfeld & Nicholson, London, 2013)

17. See Bruce Weber's article: *Charis Wilson, Model and Muse, Dies at 95, in 'New York Times' newspaper (24 November 2009).*

18. For example, Carrà G, Cazzullo C.L, Clerici M: *The association between expressed emotion, illness severity and subjective burden of care in relatives of patients with schizophrenia. Findings from an Italian population, in 'BMC Psychiatry' (BioMed Central, Open Access Publisher, 13 September 2012)*

19. *Google Suzanne Goldenberg's article: Lester Brown "Vast dust bowls threaten tens of millions with hunger" in 'The Guardian' newspaper (25 February 2015)*

20. *Quotation from* Katherine Slusher's book: 'The Green Memories of Desire: Lee Miller and Roland Penrose' (Prestel, 2007)

21. Kelly, Jain (ed), 'NUDE: THEORY' (Lustrum Press New York, 1979). Contributors: Harry Callahan, Lucien Clergue, Ralph Gibson, Kenneth Jose Manuel Alvarez Bravo, Duane Michals, Helmut Newton, *et al*

22. For example, see Naomi Gryn's article: *Why I'm having my first baby at 51'*, in 'The Guardian' newspaper (9 November 2012)

23. Google William Boyd's article: *Egon Schiele: a graphic virtuoso rescued from the wilderness* in 'The Guardian' newspaper (10 October 2014)

24. See Marie-Laure Bernadac's essay in: Baer B, Bernadac M-L, Leiris M, Richardson J, Scarpetta G, Sylvester D: 'Le Dernier Picasso 1953 - 1973' (MNAM/Centre Georges Pompidou, Paris, 1988)

25. See Kimberley Bradley's article: *Wally Neuzil – the secret life of Schiele's muse*, in 'The Guardian' newspaper (27 February 2015)

26. See the chapter by Helmut Newton in: Kelly, Jain (ed), 'NUDE: THEORY' (Lustrum Press New York, 1979). Other contributing photographers include Harry Callahan, Lucien Clergue, Ralph Gibson, Kenneth Jose Manuel Alvarez Bravo, Duane Michals, etc.

27. Bel's fictional movie about Trish Little's project is based on a genuine 5-minute film about the work of UK artist Patricia Oxley who blogs at *isitart.co*. The movie was made by photographer Michael Kilyon. This may be viewed online at *vimeo.com/89545456*, and with Chinese subtitles at *vimeo.com/112275905*

28. See Carolyn Burke's biography: 'Lee Miller: on both sides of the camera' (Bloomsbury, London, 2006)

29. Google Tim Lott for his article *Why you shouldn't tell children they can be whatever they want*, in 'The Guardian' newspaper (7 August 2015)

30. From the home page of *sukithelifemodel.co.uk* you may read all three books of Suki's autobiographical trilogy: 'A small life,' 'Two Small lives', and 'True life nude'. These were originally serialised consecutively online over three years. Print versions of each are also available from *Amazon.com* etc.

31. Suki's poetry collections include: 'Kunst' (Indigo Dreams Publishing, England, 2012), and a joint collection with Sue Vickerman: 'Thin bones like wish-bones' (Indigo Dreams Publishing, England, 2013).

32. You will find 21 collaborative movies online made by Bel with (or about, or for) Suki, at: *vimeo.com/belphotography*

33. UK artist and theatre director Douglas Black has provided the images used for the fictitious character of Greg-I'm-a-Kiwi. See *dougalterego.blogspot.co.uk* and ***facebook.com/junglemunkey***

34. Quotation from Peter Lacey's book 'The history of the nude in photography' (Bantam Books, New York, 1964)

35. UK-based Australian artist Helen Wheatley's website is at: *helenwheatley.co.uk*

36. 'Under the gaze', Bel's 27-minute film, may be viewed online at vimeo.com/56787981, and with Chinese subtitles at *vimeo.com/121244261*

37. See article by Suzanne Goldenberg: *Lester Brown: "Vast dust bowls threaten tens of millions with hunger"* in 'The Guardian' newspaper (25 February 2015)

38. See J.G. Ballard's book 'Miracles of Life: Shanghai to Shepperton: an Autobiography' (Harper Collins, London, 2014)

39. Quotation from the novel by Yu Hua: ‚China in Ten Words' (Gerald Duckworth & Co, UK, 2012)

40. See the article by Pankaj Mishra: *How to think about Islamic State*, in 'The Guardian' newspaper (25 July 2015)

41. On Youtube, search for Chopin nocturne 19 in E Minor, op. 72/1 (posth.) B.19

42. See Sara Ziff's article: *Yes, you should feel bad for models: we're being told to go diet – or go broke* in 'The Guardian' newspaper (9 September 2014)

43. The full text of 'Crossing Boundaries – an interview with Nobuyoshi Araki' may be found online at:
dpreview.com/forums/thread/3654593

44. Twenty-two photographs by Lee Miller are included in a book edited by Ernestine Carter: 'Grim Glory: London Under Fire' (Lund Humphries / Scribners, London, 1941)

45. See Cook, Rachel: *Women at war: Lee Miller exhibition includes unseen images of conflict* in 'The Observer' newspaper, 19 September 2015

46. See Becky E. Conekin's book 'Lee Miller in Fashion' (Thames and Hudson 2013)

47. Bel's movie 'Qi Qi's Life Room' may be viewed online with English & Chinese subtitles at this link: https://vimeo.com/119526858

48. 'Kunst' poetry collection by Suki (Indigo Dreams Publishing, England, 2012)

49. Bel made the 6-minute movie 'Still Life' based on 'A small life', Part I of Suki's autobiographical trilogy. 'Still Life' may be viewed online at *vimeo.com/124501563* and with Chinese subtitles at *vimeo.com/124499437*.

50. Read Suki's poem 'Running Joke' on page 25 of 'Thin bones like wish-bones' by Suki and Sue Vickerman (Indigo Dreams Publishing, England, 2013)

51. Google this article by Jonathan Jones: *The $6.5m canyon: it's the most expensive photograph ever – but it's like a hackneyed poster in a posh hotel,* in 'The Guardian' newspaper (10 December 2014)

52. You will find this poem on page 64 of 'Thin bones like wish-bones' by Suki and Sue Vickerman (Indigo Dreams Publishing, England, 2013)

Bibliography and film references

Books

Baer B, Bernadac M-L, Leiris M, Richardson J, Scarpetta G, Sylvester D: 'Le Dernier Picasso 1953 - 1973' (MNAM/Centre Georges Pompidou, Paris, 1988)

Ballard, J.G.: 'Miracles of Life: Shanghai to Shepperton: an Autobiography' (Harper Collins, London, 2014)

Burke, Carolyn: 'Lee Miller: on both sides of the camera' biography (Bloomsbury 2006)

Carter, Angela: *The Sadeian Woman: An Exercise in Cultural History'* (Virago, London, 1979)

Carter, Ernestine (ed): 'Grim Glory: London Under Fire' (Lund Humphries / Scribners, London, 1941)

Chu, Ben: 'Chinese whispers – why everything you've heard about China is wrong' (Weidenfeld & Nicholson, London, 2013)

Conekin, Becky E: 'Lee Miller in Fashion' (Thames and Hudson 2013)

Hua, Yu: 'China in ten words' novel (Pantheon, New York, 2011)

Kelly, Jain (ed), 'NUDE: THEORY' (Lustrum Press New York, 1979). Contributors: Harry Callahan, Lucien Clergue, Ralph Gibson, Kenneth Jose Manuel Alvarez Bravo, Duane Michals, Helmut Newton, *et al*

Kleinfelder, Karen L: 'The Artist, His Model, Her Image, His Gaze' (University of Chicago Press 1993)

Lacey, Peter: 'The history of the nude in photography' (Bantam Books, New York, 1964)

Maddow, Ben; Weston, Edward: 'Edward Weston: Seventy Photographs', biography (New York Graphic Society, Boston, 1979)

Masoch, Leopold: 'Venus in Furs' new edition (Penguin Classics, London, 2000)

Prose, Francine: 'The lives of the muses: nine women and the artists they inspired' (Union Books, 2013)

Raven, Langer, Frueh (eds): Feminist Art Criticism: an anthology (UMI Research Press, Ann Arbor, 1988)

Slusher, Katherine: 'The Green Memories of Desire: Lee Miller and Roland Penrose' (Prestel, 2007)

Sontag, Susan: 'On Photography' (Penguin, London, 1979)

Vickerman, Sue, & Suki: 'Thin bones like wish-bones', poetry collection (Indigo Dreams Publishing, England, 2013)

Wilson, Charis; Madar, Wendy: 'Through another lens: my years with Edward Weston' (North Point Press, USA, 1999)

Articles about art and artists

Bernadac, Marie-Laure: *Picasso 1953-1972: Painting as Model* in Britt D. (tr): 'Late Picasso' [The Tate Gallery, London, 1988], 1989.

Boyd, William: *Egon Schiele: a graphic virtuoso rescued from the wilderness* – a review in 'The Guardian' newspaper (10 October 2014)

Bradley, Kimberley: *Wally Neuzil – the secret life of Schiele's muse*, in 'The Guardian' newspaper (27 February 2015)

Cook, Rachel: *Women at war: Lee Miller exhibition includes unseen images of conflict* in 'The Observer' newspaper (19 September 2015). To view some of these photographs online, go to:

theguardian.com/artanddesign/gallery/2015/sep/19/lee-millers-stunning-images-of-women-in-wartime-in-pictures

Doyle, Sady: *Before Lena Dunham, there was Anaïs Nin – now patron saint of social media,* in 'The Guardian' newspaper (7 April 2015)

Jones, Jonathan: *The \$6.5m canyon: it's the most expensive photograph ever – but it's like a hackneyed poster in a posh hotel,* in 'The Guardian' newspaper (10 December 2014)

O'Hagan, Sean*: Photography is Art and always will be,* 'The Guardian' newspaper (11 December 2014)

Searle, Adrian: *Ai Weiwei review – momentous and moving,* in 'The Guardian' newspaper (14 September 2015)

Searle, Adrian: *Must try softer ,* a criticism of the art of Euan Uglow in 'The Guardian' newspaper (8 July 2003)

Weber, Bruce: *Charis Wilson, Model and Muse, Dies at 95, in 'New York Times' newspaper (24 November 2009)*

Ryan, Fergus: *Chinese mock claims Beijing is most liveable city despite smog lifting,* in 'The Guardian' newspaper (22 August 2015)

Ziff, Sara: *Yes, you should feel bad for models: we're being told to go diet – or go broke* in 'The Guardian' newspaper (9 September 2014)

Articles about life and society

Carrà G, Cazzullo C.L, Clerici M: *The association between expressed emotion, illness severity and subjective burden of care in relatives of patients with schizophrenia. Findings from an Italian population, in 'BMC Psychiatry' (BioMed Central, Open Access Publisher, 13 September 2012)*

Goldenberg, Suzanne: *Lester Brown "Vast dust bowls threaten tens of millions with hunger"* in 'The Guardian' newspaper (25 February 2015)

Gryn, Naomi: *Why I'm having my first baby at 51,* in 'The Guardian' newspaper (9 November 2012)

Lott, Tim: *Why you shouldn't tell children they can be whatever they want,* in 'The Guardian' newspaper (7 August 2015)

Mishra, Pankaj: *How to think about Islamic State,* in 'The Guardian' newspaper (25 July 2015)

Verhaegen, Paul: *Neo-liberalism brings out the worst in us,* in 'The Guardian' newspaper (29 September 2014)

Films

'Under the gaze' (2012)
Bel's 27-minute film is partly biographical about Suki, and otherwise addresses the 'male gaze' debate instigated by Laura Mulvey in the 1970s.
vimeo.com/56787981
vimeo.com/121244261 (with Chinese subtitles)

'The Life Room No.8 - Patricia Oxley' (2014)
This is a five-minute film about the work of UK artist Patricia Oxley made by photographer Michael Kilyon. The fictional movie by 'Bel' about the art project of 'Trish Little' is based on this film.
vimeo.com/89545456
vimeo.com/112275905 (with Chinese subtitles)

'Qi Qi's Life Room' (2015)
Bel's five-minute movie (with Chinese-English subtitles) is part of her 'Life Room' series.
https://vimeo.com/119526858